AUTUMN IN BRANDFORD

Lyn Corvet

AUTUMN IN BRANDFORD
Copyright © 2023 by Lyn Corvet
All rights reserved.
Published by Lyn Corvet in The United States
No parts of this publication may be reproduced, stored in a retrieval system, or transmitted in any form or by any means, electronic, mechanical, photocopying, recording, or otherwise, without the prior written permission of the copyright owner.
This is a work of fiction. Any similarity between the characters and situations within its pages and places or persons, living or dead, is unintentional and co-incidental.
Cover Photography
Cover Design by Lyn Corvet and
ISBN: 978-1-0882-7739-3

DEDICATION

This book is dedicated to Deb,

the first person to fall in love with Mena, Chase and Brandford Beach.
Thank you!

CHAPTER ONE

Wilhelmina Prescott found herself entranced by the beautiful shade of blue the September sky had become over this particular parcel of land in West Chester, Pennsylvania. It couldn't have been more perfect. It was the color that an artist would choose to convey a landscape meant to evoke peace and happiness from anyone that studied it.

She stood quietly, hands clasped in front of her, noticing that everything was in on the act. The grass was like blades constructed out of the most precious jade stone. The leaves left no brilliant color unrepresented.

Everything about Mena's surroundings was nothing short of visual perfection. With one glaring exception.

She looked back at the casket covered with flowers, and fresh tears glistened on her lashes.

This beautiful day was the day that she would say her final goodbye to Christopher D'Angelo.

Mena, her husband Tyler, and their eighteen year old daughter Gemma had made the trip back home to Pennsylvania from Connecticut when she'd received word of her grandfather's passing. Her family's demeanor was as she had expected. They weren't only distant because of the two states that now separated them. They'd grown distant long before Mena had moved away. So she kept to herself, lost in her own cloud of sadness and regret. When Tyler reached for her hand to offer support, she pulled it away. But when her daughter slid her arm through Mena's, she leaned into her. So glad that she had decided to come along.

After the service Mena wanted to run to the car, but knew that wasn't an option. For some unknown reason, when Mena was a teenager, her mother had made the familial decree that they were to no longer have a relationship with her parents. Mena's grandparents. There were never any details given as to why this was the way things had to be, and by the time Mena was an adult she was too focused on her own life to give it much more thought. But as she stood at the graveside, she was sure that she was the only one feeling any guilt or regret that fences hadn't been mended when there had still been time. It seemed as if her family attended because it was what was expected, but no one shed a tear. There were no conversations that Mena overheard about Christopher. Only talks about where they were going after the service, whose kids had to go where, and even if one's car had enough gas to get home.

Her family. She wished she could pinpoint exactly when they'd completely fallen apart. Or maybe she had just dreamed up an alternate childhood, and in reality her family had always been this way.

She sighed. Her brain was too tired to think about it anymore.

"Aunt incoming," Gemma whispered, seeing her aunt saying her goodbyes to Gemma's grandparents and uncle.

Then came, "Willie, I can't believe you came," Priscilla said as she approached Mena's family. "I figured you'd just ask us how it was at Christmas," she added with a laugh.

"Hi Aunt Priscilla," Gemma said, giving her aunt a smile that spoke of the protection she was ready and willing to offer her mother if necessary.

"Hi Gem." Priscilla's eyes turned back to her little sister. "So are you going to Shawn's house for lunch?"

Mena shook her head.

"I have to get back to school," Gemma answered, her arm tightening around her mother's.

Priscilla nodded. "Well, it would have been nice to have you join us, but I can't say I'm surprised that you're jetting out of town already. Are you even going to say hi to Mom and Dad, or Shawn?"

"I talked to everyone, Priscilla," Mena said quietly. "And I'll make sure I get down again before the holidays. But like Gemma said, we have to get her back to school."

Again, Priscilla nodded. "Okay then. Well ... have a safe trip. I'll give everyone your goodbyes."

"I gave them to them myself," Mena said, but forced a smile. "It's nice to see you Priscilla. In person, and not just on Facebook." Her sister lived her life for likes and comments. Creating an online existence that didn't very closely resemble her somewhat uneventful reality. No doubt trying to recapture the attention she'd received when she was younger.

"Are you on Facebook? I never see you comment on any of my posts," Priscilla said with a phony smile of her own.

"We have to go, Priscilla. I'll call you this week," Mena said. She waved to the smaller groups of her family that still stood closer to the graveside. A few returned the wave, others just looked on, leaning in to comment to whoever was next to them.

Mena started her walk back to the car. To peace and safety. Tyler and Gemma on either side of her.

"Not a warm and friendly bunch," Tyler commented as they walked. "I mean I know it's a funeral but man ... talk about a chilly reception."

"Tyler, please don't," Mena whispered as she watched a man walking across the perfectly manicured grass. She was surprised when he came straight for her as she thought she recognized him as her grandfather's lawyer.

"Wilhelmina?" he asked. "You're Christopher's granddaughter?"

Mena nodded. "I am. And you're his ... lawyer?"

"Yes." He extended his hand. "Jason Milstead. I'd like to speak with you privately if you have a moment. My office is only a few blocks away. Would you have time before you head back home?"

Mena looked at him, confused. "Are you sure you don't want to talk to my mother? I think she's handling everything."

He smiled. "No, this is something I need to speak to you about."

Mena glanced at her husband and daughter, who both nodded, and then answered with, "Okay. Sure."

"Would you like to walk?" Jason asked.

"We'll drive if you don't mind. That way we don't have to come back here ..."

"Of course. I understand." He pointed to the left. "My address is 15

Madison so you just go down this road, turn right and I'm on the left. I'll be right there."

Mena nodded. "Thank you." She glanced over her shoulder and saw most of her family looking at her. She knew they were all chomping at the bit to know why her grandfather's lawyer would need to speak to her. But instead of speaking to them again she simply continued on to the car, getting into the passenger seat. She just looked up at the blue sky, waiting for her husband to get in and start the engine.

When he did just that, he turned and looked at her with a smile. "What do you think he wants to talk to you about? Did your grandfather have some money hidden away, do you think?"

"Don't, Tyler," Mena whispered. "Please."

"Okay, but it's kind of exciting. Don't you think so?"

"No. I don't," was another whisper.

It was a quick drive to 15 Madison, parking along the curb directly in front of the home that had been converted into a lawyer's office, with what appeared to be apartments above.

"I'll just go in by myself," Mena said, opening her door.

"What? Why?" Tyler asked. "I want to go in with you." He got out of the car and hurried around to stand beside his wife.

She looked at her husband and shook her head ever so slightly. She lowered her voice to keep Gemma from hearing her words. "Ty, I appreciate you driving me down here today but ... let's not pretend that we're okay. I can't ... I need to go in by myself."

"Mee--"

"Ty, please. I can't right now. I'm sure I won't be long." She looked around. "There's a café right over there. Why don't you get us something to eat for the road?"

Gemma got out of the back seat and quickly said, "No worries, Mom. We'll go get food and you just ... take your time. We're here if you need us."

Mena gave her daughter a smile. She knew that the only reason she had made the trip to Pennsylvania was to run interference for Mena. Interference with her family, and interference with Tyler. Now, she was doing just that.

Tyler nodded, still clearly not happy with her decision. "Okay. Let's go kiddo."

"Thank you," Mena said before closing the car door and walking toward the building's entrance. She turned to watch Tyler and Gemma cross the street and go inside the diner.

"Hey, good timing!"

She jumped just a little.

Jason was walking toward her. "Sorry to scare you. I thought you saw me."

"No, it's fine. I was just ... lost in thought, I guess," Mena answered.

"Well, here, let me get that," he said, opening the door.

She walked into a rather small office, stepping aside so that Jason could walk around her, closing the door behind him.

"I could tell by your expression at the cemetery that you weren't expecting anything from your grandfather," he said, going around his desk and sitting down, shuffling files and papers on the desktop until he found the manila envelope he was looking for. "But I was under strict orders to give you this upon his passing. I was to do it in private, away from any other family members." He handed the envelope out to her. When she took it slowly, he also handed her one of his business cards. "And please take this in case you have any questions."

She reached for his card. "So you know what's in here?" she asked softly.

He nodded. "I drew everything up for Christopher."

"Did he talk to you about me?" was her next softly spoken question.

"He did. A little. He would always joke that he didn't want us to talk too much because it made me take too long and charge him more," Jason said with a smile.

"That sounds like the grandfather I remember," she whispered.

"Well like I said, if you have any questions after going through the envelope, I'm here to help you in any way that I can."

"Thank you," Mena said, holding tightly to the envelope. "I will." She turned for the door.

"My condolences to you, Wilhelmina. Christopher was a good man," Jason said behind her.

She nodded before opening the door and stepping back out into the late summer sunlight.

CHAPTER TWO

     Mena felt the soft, warm breeze blow against her face from the open window. She sat in her bedroom chair, hearing the rustling of the trees, but only seeing her own memories. Memories dusted in a golden hue as they danced around before her. Her childhood. Her family. Her happiness.

     She picked up the letter again that had been among the contents of the envelope the lawyer had given to her. She once again read her grandfather's words, written in the shaky handwriting of the eighty-two year old man:

My sweet Willie,

I'm sure you're surprised to get this letter. My doctor told me that I needed to get my affairs in order. Sadly, there is not much that needs tending to. Regardless of the strained relationship I've had with your mother she will still inherit my house and its contents to do with as she wishes. I sense a yard sale in her future. But to you I am leaving the only possession I have that truly means anything to me. The beach house. I know that you thought it was sold so long ago, but I have held on to it all of these years. Accumulating some of the best memories of my lifetime. Sadly, the rather sudden onset of my illness left me unable to go back one last time and pack up everything

that I kept there, so I am hoping that you would do that for me. I guess afterwards you can do what you want with everything. I'd just feel better knowing a stranger wasn't going through my house. I know that things got in the way of our relationship but I never stopped loving you, my amazing granddaughter. I want nothing but happiness for you and hope that maybe, in some small way, the Brandford Beach cottage can help you find it. As it did for me. You might have thought that I'd lived a long enough life to leave nothing undone or unsaid, but it's not true. So please learn from my mistakes and don't let that happen to you. I've always loved you.
    Pop

    She wiped the tears from her cheeks as her other hand just ran lightly over the paper. "I'm so sorry," she whispered. "You deserved so much better from me."

    "Mom?"

    Mena quickly wiped the tears from her cheeks again and turned to see her daughter standing in the open doorway. "Hi sweetheart," she said softly.

    "Is it okay if I come in?" Gemma asked, respecting her mother's need for privacy at such an emotional time.

    "Of course. Yes. Come in."

    The young woman walked across the soft carpet to sit in the chair near her mother's. "Is there anything I can do?" she asked.

    Mena shook her head. "I hadn't even seen my grandfather since before you were born …" The realization that the chance for her grandfather to ever see her daughter was now gone, hit her so painfully. The opportunity was buried along with his body in that cemetery.

    "I don't have to go back to school," Gemma offered. "I can stay here with you. Just … hang out."

    "I love you for saying that. But no. I want you to go back to school. It means everything to me that you took this time and came home to be there with me. Really."

    Gemma nodded toward the open envelope and paper laying in her mother's lap. "What are you going to do about the house?" she asked softly.

Mena shook her head, the memories once again a dull noise playing out in her mind. "I don't know. I didn't even know he still had it. He said he'd sold it before you were born. And … why leave it to me?"

"Maybe it's his way of .... mending that fence that was broken for so long," Gemma suggested.

"But the whole rest of my family is in Pennsylvania. I'm up here in Connecticut. Taking care of his beach home in Delaware is not really ... convenient."

"Whatever happened between the two of you anyway?" Gemma asked softly.

"It wasn't so much me that it happened to. Something happened between Mom and him, and I ... sided with my mother. I was young and couldn't imagine my mother being wrong about anything. She didn't need to tell me why we weren't speaking to him anymore. I had her back." Mena paused for a moment. "And then I got older and realized that my mother wasn't always right when it came to how she handled her relationships. The last few years I was thinking about how I wanted to reach out to my grandfather but ... I waited too long. I kept putting it off as things got a little more ... confused around here and ..." She shrugged, tears glistening in her eyes. "But I mean he didn't reach out to me either, right?"

Gemma put her hand on her mother's knee. "I don't know anything about your grandfather, but I know that there isn't a better person or mother in the world than you. So ... please don't beat yourself up about anything. And you know what? You can just call a realtor and have them put it on the market. You can sign everything electronically these days. You don't even have to go to Delaware. I think that's what you should do. I don't want you going there. I don't think it would be good for you right now. You're already dealing with so much emotionally, and I don't like seeing you like this. This funeral ... the letter ... You look so sad, Mom. I'm worried about you."

Mena shook her head again. "I'll be okay. There's just so much going on inside of my head right now, you know? But even with everything else, I can put it all aside and do this one thing. I can fulfill my grandfather's final wish. Go to Brandford and pack up his belongings. And then ...," she shrugged. " ...   do whatever I want with it," she said softly. "That doesn't sound too hard. He said he wanted me to be happy and thought the cottage could do that. Which I guess means he was kind of hoping I would want to keep it. Unless he thought packing up his things would be what would make me happy." She gave Gemma the hint of a smile. All she could muster.. "But I don't even know if it's inhabitable. It really wasn't the last time I saw it. I guess I'll take a sleeping bag just in case. I don't think even a cottage as small as his could be cleaned out in a day."

"You never talked about it. What was it like? The house. That beach?" Gemma asked.

"It was ... boring. Or that's what my younger self thought."

"How old were you?"

"I don't think we went much after I was seven or eight."

"Why was it boring?"

Mena was quiet for a moment, hearing her and her sister singing Mockingbird on the little, sand covered porch at Brandford Beach. There was the ghost of a smile on her face as she started to introduce her daughter to these memories. "I am embarrassed now to say that first and foremost, I was embarrassed then of the house, the beach, everything. My friends were going to beaches with boardwalks, amusement piers, concerts ... while this beach had a country store. That was it. The house, it was just a tiny little cottage, a shack, and it was always in some stage of repair. My grandfather was always fixing it up, or so he'd say. But really he was just slowly dismantling the insides. So here it was, surrounded by beautiful homes, but we'd pull up with our jugs of water just so that we could flush the toilet ..." She paused, the air from her open window turning into the air that would come up the sand covered road from the water. "But," she said quietly, "I also remember the small black and silver radio that my dad would take down so that he could listen to the baseball games. Harry Kalas calling the action. And my grandparents always had a cooler of store brand soda cans: orange, grape, root beer, cola, birch beer ..."

"Sounds kind of nice to me, Mom," Gemma said.

"Yeah ... It does, doesn't it? But I never appreciated it back then. I didn't know how quickly time would move on and it would all be gone. The days, the people, the relationships, the songs, ... it's all just memories now. Why was I in such a hurry to grow up? To go to places that I was so obnoxious to think were better? Everything I ever needed was right there." She gave her daughter a sad smile. "I sound like Dorothy, don't I?"

Gemma smiled. "There's no place like home." She stood up and then leaned over to place a kiss on her mother's cheek. "Do you want to come down for dinner or should I bring something up for you?"

"Would you mind bringing something up? But not much, please. I'm not too hungry," Mena whispered, once again turning her eyes to the window and the memories that played like a movie just beyond.

"You're really going to do this?" Tyler Prescott asked his wife as she continued packing her suitcase.

"Ty, can we please not fight about this again? Yes, I'm doing it. I'm going to go and handle this for my grandfather. And I think it will do us both good to have this time apart. To ... figure out what we're going to do."

Tyler walked over to the bed, putting his hand on her arm. "How many more times can I say how sorry I am? It was the one time. That's all. If I could go back and change things ..."

Mena took a step to the side to try to have his hand drop from her arm, not wanting to be touched. "Please don't lie to me anymore, Ty," she said softly. "I want off of this particular merry go round of a conversation. One person doesn't equate to one time. You can't even be honest with me. I wouldn't have even known about your affair if I hadn't seen those texts. I'd still be thinking everything was perfect. No wonder you think I'm an idiot--"

"How can you say that? I would never think anything even close to that. You're the smartest person I know."

Mena just looked at him for a moment before shaking her head and then zipping up her suitcase. "I'm going to take Gemma back to school and then drive to Delaware. I'll let you know when I get there. It should be about five or six hours I'm thinking."

"Mena," Tyler said emotionally. "Please. Just tell me what I can do."

She lifted her suitcase off of the bed and started for the door. "Maybe don't have your secretary over while I'm gone," she said without looking back. But then she stopped and turned back to face him. "I'm sorry. Just ... give me this time. That's what you can do."

"And then we'll be okay?" Tyler asked as she opened the bedroom door.

She looked at him for a few seconds and then took her bags down the stairs and out to the car where her daughter was already waiting.

The two women had driven almost half the way in silence. Not an uncomfortable silence, but one where a person just wants to make sure every second is committed to memory. Finally, it was Gemma that spoke.

"Do you think you and Daddy are going to get a divorce?" she asked.

"I don't know, sweetheart. I'm sorry. I wish I could give you a definitive 'no', but ... I think I need to get everything with my grandfather taken care of before I can really just sit and … try to figure everything else out. Which probably makes no sense to you. You're so young and … he's your father. I know how hard it must be to see us as anything other than your parents."

"No, Mom. I get it," Gemma said with a hint of a sad smile. "I've heard the fighting. Even though you always tried to keep your voice down. He didn't. It made me so sad. I don't understand how he could have done that to you. To us. And for you to find out the way you did … You have always been the best Mom … the best person I know."

Mena glanced over at her daughter with a smile. "Thank you, honey, but I'm far from perfect and all marriages have their ups and downs. But if you lose the trust that should be the cornerstone of your relationship …. I don't know how you go on together. I would never have done that to your father. It's so foreign to me." She couldn't bring herself to tell her daughter that in her heart she already knew that she couldn't stay in the marriage. She didn't want to hurt her. So she kept trying to pretend that there was a way to fix it all. "In my family. Finding out that my grandfather had lied about selling the beach house is probably the worst lie hanging in the branches of our family tree. Well if we don't count just being awful people," she said, trying to put on another smile.

Gemma couldn't help but laugh softly. "Why do you really think he did that?"

Mena shook her head slightly. "I have no idea. It is a really strange thing to lie about for almost thirty years."

"Are you sure you don't want me to go with you? I can wait a few days to go back to school."

"Absolutely not," Mena said. "This is your first year of college. This is your time to spread your wings, Gem. As soon as you get out of this car I want you to forget all of this family bullshit going on and … enjoy being eighteen. Enjoy your freedom, and enjoy knowing that your entire life is gift wrapped right in front of you. Just waiting to be opened."

Gemma watched her mother's profile. "Are you sorry that you married Daddy?" she asked quietly.

"What? No. Of course not. Your father gave me you! And we were happy for a very long time. And maybe we'll find a way to work all of this out and be happy again. I don't know. But I do know there are zero regrets about choosing the path that gave me my most precious gift. My daughter.

My friend."

Gemma leaned over and kissed her mother's cheek. "I love you, Mom. Please be okay," she whispered. "And call me if you just want to talk. I'm afraid you're going to be sad. And lonely."

It was late September so the summer visitors would mostly have disappeared from Brandford Beach.

"Are you going to be alright?" Gemma asked.

Mena nodded. "Absolutely. I'll send you lots of pictures."

"Promise?"

"Cross my heart," Mena answered as the car came to a stop in front of Gemma's dorm. "Please don't worry about me. I'm good. I think I need this. I really do. It's going to be good for me. Maybe the place will just need a new makeover. It's been so long since I've done any design work."

"That would be so great!" Gemma said. "I know how much you loved doing that.."

"Well I loved being a mom more, and your father wanted me home so ... I was happy. And selling my business put a nice nest egg in the bank."

Gemma took off her seat belt and leaned over to hug her mother tightly. "I love you, Mom. So much!" she whispered. "Whatever you need to do to be happy ... with your marriage, or going back to work ... I support you."

Mena returned the hug, placing a kiss against her daughter's auburn hair. "Thank you. But you'll never be asked to choose sides in any of this. I promise you that much."

"I know you wouldn't do that to me, but still ... you've got me. No matter what."

"And that means more to me than you could ever know," Mena said softly.

"Call me later?" Gemma asked as she opened her door.

"As soon as I get to the house. A picture and a phone call."

"Listen to good music," Gemma said as she took her backpack and bag from the backseat.

"Oh I have my seventies playlist ready to go. Five hours of memories and music," Mena said with a smile. "I'll be singing at the top of my lungs. You know it's true."

Gemma smiled as she leaned in the open window of the now closed passenger side door. "I love you, Mom," she said, reaching in to grasp her mother's hand.

"I love you, my angel," Mena responded, giving her daughter's hand a squeeze before letting go. She watched her daughter walk away before starting the car again, and beginning the next leg of her journey to Brandford Beach.

CHAPTER THREE

Meena's drive to Delaware had seemed to fly by so quickly, with the mist of her memories keeping her company. But now she looked around and everything was completely different. The landmarks that she remembered from this trip as a girl were no longer there. Replaced instead by a highway that cut through the beautiful, small towns so that more people could get to the string of beaches more quickly. As she drove, she couldn't help but think about her place in the middle of the back seat of the Chevy Impala station wagon. Trying to keep her feet balanced on the center hump on the floor. If one of her feet went off she'd have a brother holler at her on her left, or a sister holler at her on the right. Sometimes she'd ride in the back with a soft blanket and pillow. It was those times that the trip could take forever and she wouldn't have minded. Her parents both loved music, so the radio was always on. Except if they traveled on the weekends, in which case the Phillies game would be playing. Her brother Shawn would eagerly be asking questions about what he was hearing. Her and her sister talking softly about the music they weren't hearing, or their favorite subject: boys.

So many songs took Mena back to those two hour trips. Her song memories were categorized from her youth. There were songs that she loved back then and purchased with her allowance to play over and over at home.

There were songs that she liked but could do with just hearing them on the radio. And then there were songs that she didn't particularly like back then, but now, to hear them, was like looking at a snapshot of those summers. Her mother's frosted blonde hair and shimmering pink lipstick. Her father's bearded profile as he'd steal glances over at his beautiful wife.

Mena put on her turn signal to make the left onto Brandford Road. When she was young she always got excited thinking they were finally at the beach. But each and every time she was quickly reminded that this road wound its way through trees and lakes, taking its time before finally opening up to the familiar beach, at the intersection where the small country store stood for so long.

When she reached that intersection where the store still sat, she pulled straight ahead and then into one of the few parking spaces along the left hand side of the parking lot, unable to believe that here, everything looked exactly the same as she remembered. She turned off the car and got out, bringing just her keys and phone with her. She started walking across the sand covered blacktop to where the sandy beach began only a few yards away. She stood at the edge of the rocky sand, looking out toward the water. How many times had she stood here as a child? Ice cream cone or green apple flavored gumballs in hand. Her eyes teared up as she thought about how all of those memories were now decades old, and the family she had shared them with was as fractured as a family could be. Now the family of her own that came after was fracturing too, right before Mena's eyes.

She took a deep breath and let it out slowly before returning to her car and climbing back in. She made her way the half mile to the sandy road where her grandfather's cottage could be found. The road had only four homes on it. Two on each side. Her grandfather's was the second one on the left hand side. The only one of the four that hadn't been remodeled or updated to hold up better against the storms that were so frequent during this time of year. Two of the homes appeared to be closed up for the season, but the one across the way from her grandfather's seemed to still be occupied.

She pulled her car up in front of the cottage and looked sadly at its condition. The dark red paint was chipping off of the wood and cinder block exterior. The screens of the front porch were ripped and flapping in the slight breeze. Nature had also taken over the small lot. Any landscaping that might have once been done was now buried beneath the native plants and trees that had pushed their way through the sand.

Mena turned off the engine and got out of the car. She wondered to herself if she'd even be able to stay here. It obviously needed more than just a makeover. What if the inside was even worse than the outside? She couldn't see the roof or back wall. What if one or both had caved in?

She took a deep breath and pushed her way through the brush, pulling open the screen door to the concrete porch. She felt a little claustrophobic, her hand shaking as she put the key up to the deadbolt lock that had been placed in the door above the small door knob. The key didn't want to immediately turn but after applying just a little more strength she felt the release of the lock. She reached down and turned the knob, pushing the door open.

As a child, this door had never been closed. The screens around the porch kept out the bugs, so this front door had always been pushed open. With the exception of the few times they spent the night, Mena just always thought of the doorway being an open walkway from the porch to the living area.

Tears came to her eyes as she stepped inside. Tears for her lost childhood, lost relationships, lost chances to fix what had been broken, and whatever it was that caused her grandfather to lie to his whole family about this cottage. He must have loved it so much, and now it looked like a number of animals had been calling it home for quite some time in his absence. Her heart sank as she looked around. Framed photos still sat on dust covered tables. Cobwebs now lacing their way from the objects to the tabletop or wall. It was obviously exactly how her grandfather had left it the last time he walked out and locked the door for what he thought would just be the winter season. Not knowing that he'd never return. His dishes had been cleaned and neatly stacked away. The refrigerator and cabinets had been cleaned out of any food that would not survive until his return. It was just frozen in time. Covered in sand and dust.

Mena walked around, looking past her grandfather's personal items and furniture. The walls seemed to have held up. The roof was still intact with no signs of water damage. So maybe she could just clean it up and put it on the market. If she had a sign put in the yard today, she'd be practically giving it away. But it wasn't a small financial gain that made her sad. She didn't want people seeing this tiny plot of land that meant so much to her grandfather in its current condition. It was an important place to him, so Mena made the decision right then and there that it was important to her too.

There was no denying the amount of work that was needed, but before she rolled her sleeves up and got started, she took a stroll to the hill that stood between the houses and the beach. The two story houses had views of the water, but nothing could be seen from the windows of her grandfather's little house. She looked out over the sand to the water that lapped at the shore in small, slow moving waves. Looking one way and then the other she could only make out a handful of other people still trying to get some time on this beautiful beach before packing it in for the inevitable colder weather that would be moving in soon. Mena turned her back to the water and held out her phone, giving her selfie a stunning background. She snapped a photo and quickly sent it to her daughter. She sent an accompanying text that read 'I made it safely. A lot of work to do. Going to get started. Wish me luck. I'll send more pictures later. Love you!'

She got a response back immediately from Gemma. 'Beautiful. Did you eat yet? You need to take care of yourself. Call me when you can. Love you Mom!!'

Mena stared at her phone, knowing that she had one more text to send. She quickly brought up Tyler's name and typed 'Made it. Will call in a day or two.'

She walked back down over the hill, taking a moment to look at her neighbor's beautiful home. It had been raised up as a safety precaution against hurricanes and storms. A wooden staircase led from beside the carport to a lovely deck that wrapped around the main floor. The upper floor had two sets of doors that opened up to their own small, private balconies.. Mena could only imagine how breathtaking the views must be from up there.

As she took a few more steps she stopped, a long forgotten memory coming back quickly. She turned to once again look at that house. It had been one of those rare times that her family had stayed for the night, after her grandparents had gone back home for the weekend. Once they had all gotten into bed and/or sleeping bags, it was eerily quiet. Her parents slept in the back room, her and her sister slept on the full size bed produced from the pull-out sofa, her brother slept in a sleeping bag on the floor. Everyone had been asleep for hours when red lights began flashing through the curtains, over and over. The children woke up, scared at the thought of what might be going on right outside. Shawn quickly ran and woke up his parents while the girls scrambled out of their bedding and hurried to the front windows.

A police car and an ambulance were across the small road in front of the neighbor's house. It seemed as if every light was on in the home, each window illuminated in the dark. As Mena's family watched, a stretcher was put into the back of the ambulance that then backed down the road, driving off until its lights could no longer be seen.

"Come on," Mena's father said, putting his hand on her shoulder. "Let's all go back to bed. Show's over."

The children returned to their sleeping locations when Mena heard her mother whisper to her father, "Do you think you should go over and see what's going on?"

"They don't need me over there," her father answered. "Besides, if there's something we need to know, they'll come over and tell us."

"Well maybe just sit out on the porch for a bit? Make sure that we're safe here?"

Mena's father nodded. "Okay." He kissed his wife softly and looked at the three children. "Everybody go back to sleep. We'll walk to the store in the morning for some donuts. Okay?"

"Yes!" came excitedly from the sleeping bag.

"Can I listen to my radio?" Mena asked as her father started out the front door.

He turned and nodded. "Not for long though."

"Thanks Dad," Mena said, reaching down to the floor and picking up the transistor radio that had been the previous year's Christmas present. She pushed the earphone into her ear, Sammy John's 'Chevy Van' filling her head as she closed her eyes. She didn't want to see the scary red lights and have to wonder what had happened so close to her family while they slept. The music kept her feeling safe by drowning it all out.

The next morning, as promised, Dad took the kids to the Brandford store for donuts. After Mena had hers picked out, she walked up to the counter to stand beside her father. He stopped the conversation he'd been having with the store owner, but not before Mena heard the owner say, "They took him in for questioning. Guess they think he killed him."

Her father looked down at her and gave her a smile. "Okay, looks like we're set," he said, pulling a few dollars out of his pant's pocket to lay on the counter. "Thank you," he said to the owner. "My wife's probably going to want to pack it up today so ... we'll probably see you next summer." The two men shook hands before Mena's father ushered his children out of the store. Shawn ran on ahead, Mena's sister having chosen to stay back with their mother, it left only Mena at her father's side.

"Are we leaving?" she asked, looking up at him as they walked.

Her father nodded. "I think so, princess."

"Why? It's only Saturday."

"I think your Mom wants to get back home."

Mena gave that some thought on the walk back. She knew that wasn't what it sounded like when her father talked to the store owner, but maybe she just misunderstood.

Her father had been right, and the family was packed up and left the cottage that afternoon. Their stuff had already been neatly placed in the suitcases and bags when they returned from the store. Mena sat in the back of the station wagon as it pulled away, looking at their neighbor's house, wondering what could have possibly happened in a place this quiet.

Now, so many years later, Mena was once again looking at that house. It was so different now and she was sure it was probably another family that lived there today. But the memory left her suddenly feeling so alone and isolated on that road. She finally looked away and hurried her steps back to her grandfather's cottage, knowing she had her work cut out for her if she was going to be able to sleep there tonight.

It was almost midnight when Mena finally had most of the cottage swept and dusted. She had taken the sheet off that had covered the couch and now tucked the clean sheets she brought with her around the old cushions. It was a big job accomplished for one day. Tomorrow she would start going through her grandfather's things and pack them up. She flopped down on the couch and immediately felt as if exhaustion had taken over every inch of her body. She had taken a quick video of the room and sent it to Gemma with "Goodnight!", but hadn't sent anything else to Tyler. She needed these few days away from him so that she could think. He at least owed her that much.

She slipped her feet out of her shoes and pulled her legs up onto the couch, laying down and fluffing the new pillow beneath her head. She reached up and turned off the one lamp that had been on and closed her eyes. She wasn't sure what time it was when she was awakened by the sound of a vehicle outside. She immediately felt nervous. On her first day there she had seen no one except the person working at the store. But now there was someone right outside on the road. She carefully got up off of the couch and walked slowly toward the window, just as she had done that night so long ago. She parted the curtains ever so carefully and saw the pick up truck that had pulled up in front of the house across from her. The headlights turned off and the driver's door opened. There was barely enough light for her to see the driver that got out, but she could make out that it was a man. She saw him glance at her car and then at the cottage itself. She quickly let the curtains fall back together and hurried back to the couch.

She hadn't even realized she'd fallen asleep again until she woke up in the morning, still sitting up. She rolled her head, letting out a groan at the stiffness and pain she felt.

"Oh Mena, you're too old to sleep like that," she whispered. But as soon as the memory of what had happened the night before returned, she got up off the couch and went back to the windows. The sun was out now and nothing looked as scary as it had felt the night before. There was no truck on the road any longer and it was easy to convince herself that it had all been nothing but a dream.

After brushing her teeth and pulling her hair back into a ponytail, Mena slipped on some sandals and started her walk down to the store. As she walked it was as if she could see the ghosts of her family walking along in front of her. Kids running excitedly, skipping. Not a care in the world. No cheating husband, no college tuition, no family secrets to unravel. She sang to herself as she made the walk. The songs from those carefree summers.

When she reached the store, she opened the squeaking screen door. The spring that held it caused it to snap closed quickly behind her when she let go. No one else was inside except the woman behind the counter.

"Good Morning," she called out. "You were in last night, weren't you?"

"Yes," Mena answered. "A boy ... or, young man helped me."

"Jeremy," the woman answered. "My name is Rose. I own this little place. Do you need some groceries? Or can I fix you something?" she asked.

"Could I get some coffee and an egg sandwich? And I just need to grab a few other things."

"You got it. I think you're one of our last people here. I'll even be closing up later this week. How long are you here for?" the woman asked as she went to work making Mena's sandwich.

"I'm not sure. Maybe just a few days. Maybe a little longer. I used to come all of the time when I was younger. Now it seems so quiet. Kind of eerie at nighttime."

The woman smiled. "Yeah. Most people packed up two weeks ago. Now the stragglers are packing up one by one. Which street are you?"

"Columbus."

The woman paused. "I know those four houses. Which one are you staying in?"

"I'm Christopher D'Angelo's granddaughter. Mena. Sorry. I should have introduced myself."

"Oh, that's alright," the woman said with a big smile. She seemed to be in her sixties with hair that appeared to have once been dark, now mostly a silver gray gathered into a bun. "Oh we love your grandfather around here. Haven't seen him for quite some time though. Don't think he's been down this year."

Mena paused, a half gallon of milk in her hand. "He passed away," she said softly. "That's why I'm here. To pack up his things."

The woman's sincere sadness was evident on her face immediately as she said, "Oh my gosh. I am so sorry. My heart is just broken. What a wonderful man he was. Although I'm not surprised, I guess. He was so sad when he lost ..."

"Roberta?" Mena asked. "I can only imagine how much he must have talked your ear off about my grandmother."

Rose hesitated before nodding slowly. "Your grandmother ... A very sweet woman."

Meena nodded and offered a smile, now putting her few groceries on the counter. "They were very much in love. It seems so strange to even be here with them both gone. It feels like all of my memories are still playing out like a movie or something. You know?"

The woman just nodded again, with a smile. She added a now wrapped sandwich and a cup of coffee to Mena's groceries and rang her up.

Mena handed her the money and gathered the now packed bag and coffee.

"Thank you so much, Rose," Mena said. "I'm sure I'll be seeing you again before you go."

"I look forward to it." She quickly picked up a piece of paper from the counter and put it in the top of Mena's bag. "That has our phone number on it. In case you want to call ahead for us to make you lunch. Or dinner." She handed the bag across the counter, adding, "I'm not sure if you brought your own, but if you need any boxes I have some out back. You're welcome to them."

Meena smiled. "Thank you so much!"

She walked outside, pausing when she saw that same pickup truck from the night before heading away from her, down Brandford Road. So there went her dream theory. But then where had the truck been when she'd woken up that morning?

She let the Nancy Drew questions go and made her way back to the cottage, a refreshing late summer breeze moving against her with each step. She carefully walked through the brush to the front door and went inside. The layout of the cottage was simple. On the right hand side of the front door was the kitchen area with a small table. To the left was the living room. All one big open space. Behind that area was a bathroom, a back door, and the bedroom. An average apartment had more square footage than this cozy place. It was probably built with the thought that people would be spending more time on the beach than in the house itself. This just needed as a place to change and eat.

Now Mena put her bag down on the table and took out the neatly wrapped sandwich. Along with her coffee, she took it over to the still sheet covered couch and sat down. She sat her coffee on the table beside the couch and opened the small drawer, deciding that it was as good a place to start as any. She took the drawer out and placed it beside her on the couch, unwrapping her sandwich and taking the first bite before picking up the first piece of paper from the drawer. It only had a phone number on it with a Delaware area code. She decided that a random phone number didn't need to be kept, tossing it down onto the floor to start her 'trash' pile. She took another bite of sandwich and then picked up the next thing, which was a birthday card. Someone had written "Chris" above the typed verse and beneath it was, "Love, Stevie"

Mena frowned. "Stevie? Who is Stevie?" Other than Stevie Nicks, Mena couldn't remember hearing that name discussed within her family at any time. Not that Stevie Nicks herself was discussed that often. Of course, how much did Mena really know about her grandparents' friends? She had to admit that she really didn't know much about their lives at all when they weren't with her family. So Stevie could have been a woman or a man. Part of a couple that Christopher and Roberta hung out with during their free time. Maybe it would be interesting to learn more about her grandparents. All she really knew was what she'd either seen for herself as a child, or what her mother had chosen to share with her when she was older.

The mysterious Stevie became even more mysterious as more cards were also uncovered in the drawer with that same signature. As she sipped her coffee, Mena looked at the writing, trying to determine if it looked more feminine or masculine. She couldn't really feel one way or the other as it was more a neat printing than cursive. However, it didn't go unnoticed that there were no Birthday or Thinking of You cards made out to Mena's grandmother. But maybe Christopher had already boxed up his wife's things.

Mena felt a pain in her chest as she looked at the ever growing pile of greeting cards. She could only think of her own marriage, imposing the imprint of her life onto her grandparents'. And the cards. The pain caused by discovering Tyler's infidelity made her hurt even more for her grandmother as Mena's imagination got the better of her. Did Roberta's marriage suffer from the same poison? Or did she even know? Was she also among the list of people who thought this small cottage was sold years and years ago?

Of course, there was the very real possibility that maybe all of these cards had been sent after Roberta's passing. Maybe in the final years of his life Mena's grandfather had found someone else to love.

"That's possible," Mena said quietly. But the damage had been done. At least for now. She didn't want to think anymore about Stevie and her grandfather. It made her think too much about Tyler and Nicole. Her husband wasn't even creative enough to go outside of the old 'sleeping with your secretary' trope.

Mena put down what was left of her sandwich and stood up. Most of the time when Tyler's affair came to mind, Mena was overwhelmed by a sense of disbelief. How could she have not known? They were such a happy family. Or so she thought. Tyler came home from work and was kind. Loving. He was good to Gemma. They went on vacations. Had late night dinners together. He remembered birthdays and anniversaries. Mena could have never guessed in a million years that he was also fitting an affair into his life. But he had. And now everything she thought she knew was turned upside down. Some of her friends had been supportive and told her to leave him.

"If he'd do it once, he'd do it again," Sarah, her best friend since high school, had warned her.

But others had taken a more lenient approach.

"Mena, I've seen Tyler. He looks devastated. I think he's so sorry.

I've heard Sam talking to him. I don't think he'd ever risk losing the family he loves by sleeping with anyone else ever again," Rebecca had assured her. But her loyalty was questionable given that Sam and Tyler had been friends since the second grade.

But no one could help Mena make the decision she had in front of her. To try and salvage the marriage or end it and go on alone.

She glanced back at the pile of cards. How would she feel about her grandfather if she found out he'd been having an affair too? Would it change her feelings for him? Or was it easier to forgive someone who hadn't cheated on you?

She carried her coffee back to the kitchen and sat it on the table. Then she grabbed her sunglasses and put her sandals back on. A good walk on the beach might be what she needed to clear away these distracting thoughts. Thoughts that were keeping her from getting the work at hand completed.

She closed the door behind her, carefully stepped through the weeds, and walked the short distance to the beach. There was no one else on the sand or in the water for as far as she could see. She took off her sandals, carrying them in her hand as she walked down to the water's edge, letting the small waves tickle her toes in the wet sand. It did the trick. Her mind was filled with less thoughts of extra marital affairs and more memories of her childhood. She closed her eyes as she stood there and felt as if she could open them and see her brother and sister in the water around her. She could look over her shoulder and see her mother sitting in a beach chair. Her father would be in the water. He was always the first one in and the last one out. Unless he had the grill going back at the house. Mena could almost smell his delicious hamburgers sizzling over the open flame of the cheap grill he used. Her family had been everything to Mena.

Surprisingly though, later on, Mena hadn't minded moving to Connecticut. Hours away from every member of her family. The infighting and drama that became the new norm of her family was easier to take from a distance. She found that she could have a better relationship with them if they weren't showing up at her door to 'confide' in her the things that someone else was doing to them. But strangely, she now missed them. She wanted to reach out and touch the memories of them.

With a heavy sigh she slowly started her walk back to the cottage. She looked up and saw that the beautiful blue sky was slowly being overtaken by dark clouds. She realized that she'd never been there when it rained. She wondered if it would feel even more lonely than being here in the sunshine.

It was midday when Mena heard the first rain drops. It seemed so close. As if she were in a tent rather than a cottage. As she stood looking around, at least, she thought, she'd be able to see for herself if there were any leaks anywhere.

It actually turned out to feel very cozy, the storm now sounding as if it were directly on top of her. The wind was blowing hard against the wooden exterior. Windows rattled from the combination of the wind and driving rain. Every now and then a rumble of thunder or flash of lightning would make Mena jump, but for the most part she felt safely tucked away in this seaside fortress.

Mena had a few lamps on that gave off a soft glow and some music playing from her laptop. Currently Sonny & Cher were singing about the saga of the cowboy whose work was never done.

She sat on the floor of the kitchen going through the few cabinets, removing each and every item that she found. She swayed gently to the tunes of the songs that kept her company. The same songs she would have heard on her transistor radio all of those decades ago.

As she looked around, she now had a section of the floor that was dishes and pans. There was a pile of things to throw away. Then there was a tool box that she could only imagine her grandfather must have needed quite a bit when he was staying there. She had started to open it when a loud crash from outside shook her to her core. The lights flickered before going out while her music continued, now draining her laptop's battery. She pulled herself to her feet with some help from the kitchen table before timidly going to the front window. The darkness she saw outside made her check the time on a clock that hung on the wall beside the door. She had washed it and put batteries in it earlier that day and it now told her that it was three o'clock. So why did it look like midnight?

She opened the door and could immediately feel the rain pelting her body. The screens that reached from the cinder blocks to the porch roof now just flapped against the wind. And to Mena's surprise there was also a tree that now blocked her from being able to use the door from the porch to the front yard. She momentarily panicked before remembering that there was a back door. Of course she'd have to get it taken care of. It certainly wouldn't help the resale value if a tree was sitting in the living room.

"We'll worry about that tomorrow. After all, tomorrow is another day," Mena said, doing her best Scarlett O'Hara imitation. But when she went back into the house, locking the front door behind her, she had to admit that she no longer felt quite as safe and cozy as she had earlier. The sky's black clouds were more than just a little ominous and now without the lights on she could only think about how in a few hours it would be nighttime. The start of what would no doubt be a very long night.

She went over to her laptop and turned it off, wanting to preserve the battery. She hoped this would be like the storms at home where the power would come back on before too long. But her location was remote, and most people had left. How important would restoring power to this area be to the electric company?

"Please let it be really important to you," Mena said, going over to the couch and sitting down, pulling her legs up. She sat there for several minutes before sighing. "Okay, you can still work. It's not like it's pitch black in here," she told herself. "Come on. Let's look for candles. That's probably a must have out here."

She stood back up and opened a tall metal cabinet that sat along the kitchen wall. "And here we go. Candles. Thank you, grandfather!" She gathered up the candles, placing them around the cottage. She found matches in one of the kitchen drawers and sat them on the table as well. She'd be ready for nighttime now if those lamps didn't come back on.

Having taken Rose up on her offer for the boxes earlier in the day, Mena now placed one of them on the counter and started to carefully pack some of the kitchen items inside. She made sure to leave out some things that she would need while she was there, but everything else would be put in the trunk of her car in the morning. She looked at a coffee mug that had 'I love you and coffee. But you more' written on it. She smiled as she tucked it safely into the box. Then she reached into the cabinet and pulled out another one. This one had 'Christopher's Coffee' written on it. She held that one in her hand for a moment, trying to picture her grandfather sitting out on the porch with his morning coffee. His sanctuary. His letter had said that some of his best memories were made here. Maybe something as simple as breathing in the fresh air, listening to the waves, was all that he needed to feel peace. His only child had turned her back on him and his grandchildren had chosen to not get involved. Maybe he sat on that very couch, wondering how his family had turned out to be so cruel. Maybe he came to the conclusion here that he'd been a good father and grandfather and had done all that he could for his family. Maybe this was where he decided to start living his life for nobody but himself and his wife.

She shook herself from her thoughts and wrapped the mug before putting it in the box with the others. She reached into the back of the cabinet to pull the last mug out but froze when she saw this one.

"Stevie's Coffee," she whispered as she read the writing that decorated the ceramic. Her eyes filled with tears, unable to fight her feelings any longer. Maybe it was the storm that continued to rage, or maybe it was the darkening corners of this small house, or maybe it was the realization that her own marriage was over and her life would never be the same. "Grandfather," she whispered, the mug still in her hand. "How could you do this?"

She sat the mug down on the table and went over to the couch, sitting down, hugging her pillow in front of her. Did her grandmother find out? Had she had the same confrontation with Christopher that Mena had with Tyler? Did she give him an ultimatum? Had Christopher chosen this Stevie over his wife? Mena hated herself for not having reached out more to her grandmother. She hadn't even known she was ill before getting the phone call that she had passed. She had been a terrible granddaughter. There were no two ways about it. She had abandoned the family ship for her own peace of mind. Now she laid down, still hugging her pillow, her head on the arm of the couch. She laid there crying until the exhaustion took over and, before she knew it, she was asleep.

Mena had no idea what time it was when she woke up to the sound of a chainsaw. Her first instinct was to scream. The cottage was now completely dark, so much so that Mena literally couldn't see her hand in front of her face. The sound of the saw was much too close for comfort. She felt around on the table beside her head for her phone, finally finding it. She almost instinctively turned on the flashlight but she realized at the last second that it might show through the window. She didn't want any chainsaw wielding murderers to know that she was there. Maybe even know that she was alone. So with her dark phone clutched in her hand she stood up and yet again did the timid walk to the front windows. She carefully moved the curtains only slightly to try to see outside. It was now nighttime but the moon was trying its best to offer some light through the clouds. Everything was quiet, and try as she might, Mena couldn't see any movement on the little bit of road that was visible. However, in only a few seconds the chainsaw came to life once again, and this time the tree that lay against the porch door started to move. After a moment it was no longer leaning against the cottage, having fallen to the ground. And it was then that she saw the person behind the chainsaw. Or should she say, the glowing orange tip of a cigarette that hung from the mouth of nothing more than a shadowy figure in her front yard. He must have sensed her movement, because his head turned directly toward the windows.

"Hello?" came the male voice.

Did chainsaw wielding mass murderers say hello before they killed their victims?

"I'm Chase. From across the street. Sorry if I woke you up. The rain stopped and the tree was on the house and on your car so I wanted to try and cut it up a little for you. Didn't want it going through the roof. I had knocked but there was no answer."

He stood, watching, waiting for a response that didn't come.

"I can ... go back home. If you'd rather."

Mena's brain was going a million miles an hour. But because she wasn't known for having good luck, while she stood there spying on this shadow of a man, the power came back on and she was now in the spotlight of her closest lamp. She quickly jumped out of sight, completely embarrassed.

She stood with her back against the wall, almost holding her breath.

"Hello?" he called again, but this time there was no mistaking that his voice was closer. Like maybe on the porch. "I did this for Christopher too," he then added. "Are you related to him? I'm really sorry if I overstepped."

Mena took a deep breath and let it out slowly, trying to calm her racing heart. She ran her hand quickly through her hair and then finally opened the door. She had been correct. The man was now on the porch and she could make him out more clearly.

"I'm really sorry," he said immediately. "I'm so used to being the only one here that I didn't think about how it would sound to you inside. Like the Texas Chainsaw Massacre or something."

Mena offered a little smile. "I appreciate what you did. That storm got pretty intense. I wasn't sure what I was going to do about that tree. Where did it even come from?"

Chase nodded toward the house beside Mena's cottage. "It was Ron's. Your neighbor's. I can finish cleaning it up tomorrow, if that's okay with you. And I can clear out some of this overgrowth too. If that would help."

Mena nodded. "Thank you." And then she realized that she'd never introduced herself. "I'm sorry. I'm Mena. Christopher was my grandfather."

"Mena," Chase repeated with a nod. Then he smiled. "Did you used to go by Willie? When you were little?"

Mena's eyes widened slightly. "Um … yes. When I was very little. My name is Wilhelmina. My parents started calling me Willie when I was a baby. When I got to high school I tried to get people to call me Mena. Didn't really stick with my family. But … how did you know? Did my grandfather call me Willie?"

Chase shook his head. "No. I lived across the street. Still do. I hung around with your older brother sometimes. I forgot his name?"

"Shawn."

"Right. Shawn. And you had a sister. She was … gorgeous," he added with a smile.

"She still is," Mena said. "Priscilla."

"Right!" Chase was nodding. "You guys stopped coming down. Did you move away?"

Mena looked past the man on her porch and saw that same pick up truck from the night before sitting in front of the 'murder' house. It must have belonged to him. No one else was here.

"Do you live in … that house?" she asked, pointing just a little in the direction of the beautiful home.

Chase nodded. "One of the few people here all year." He extended his hand. "Chase Harper. My grandfather built that house a long time ago. I'd live with him in the summers. My family came down on the weekends."

Mena shook his hand, noticing how handsome he was as he stood there. His dark hair hung down to his shoulders, his face showing a stubble that exposed the fact that Chase probably hadn't shaved in a few days. In the light from the cottage, Mena could also see that he was incredibly tan, and very muscular beneath his dark t-shirt. He obviously wasn't a stranger to physical work.

"I remember your family being there. I usually stuck with my family pretty much. I wasn't very sociable," she said with a smile. She wanted to ask about that night. Her family's last night at Brandford Beach. But she wasn't sure she wanted the answer just then. Not in the middle of the night. With a stranger.

As if reading her mind, Chase smiled and said, "I think I'll let you get some sleep now. The tree is off of your car and the roof so it should be okay until the morning. Again, I'm really sorry for being so … inconsiderate."

"You weren't inconsiderate. You were trying to help. And I'm very thankful." She paused before adding, "Maybe I can pick up some breakfast in the morning? We can eat before you get to work? I'll pay you. And I promise I'll help … however I can."

Chase nodded. "That sounds very nice. Thanks. But you don't have to pay me. We're neighbors. About … eight? Is that okay? Too early?"

"Eight is fine. I'll see you then. Thank you again, Chase."

"You're very welcome, Willie," Chase responded, grinning. "It's nice having somebody in here again," he added before leaving the porch and walking across the road to his house.

Mena closed the door, turning the lock before leaning back against the door frame. "Chase Harper," she whispered. "It's nice to know that gentlemen still exist." She smiled as she turned off the lamps and made her way back to the couch. The smile was still on her face when she fell asleep.

CHAPTER FOUR

When Mena's eyes opened again, the sun was now streaming in the front windows and the memories of the storm seemed more like a dream whose details were becoming harder to remember with any clarity. But the memory of Chase Harper was still crystal clear. She instantly felt guilty for admiring the look of a man that wasn't her husband, but quickly reprimanded herself. After all, she had not even come close to crossing any lines, and honestly couldn't muster up the ability to feel like she owed anything to Tyler at that moment.

She pulled herself off of the couch, this time taking the time to remove the sheet and fold it up carefully. She quickly showered, pulling her hair back into a ponytail when she was done. Then she grabbed her sunglasses, slipped into her flip flops and took off for the store. Her mind went back to that last night at the beach with her family. What had happened at the Harper place? Whatever it had been, it was bad enough that her mother had packed the family up so fast that nobody knew what hit them. Her and Mena's father had whispered most of the way home in the front seat of the station wagon, but there was nothing that Mena had been able to make out. No knowledge to be gained on the subject that was forgotten with the speed of a young girl's ever changing mind

Once she was at the store she placed her order for scrambled eggs, bacon, cinnamon rolls, and two black coffees. While she waited for the breakfast to be finished she grabbed two bottles of orange juice from the cooler and then made conversation with Rose.

"That storm was pretty wild last night."

The woman behind the counter nodded. "I was glad to see there was no damage this morning. How did you make out?"

"A tree to the roof, but other than that no harm. And … Chase Harper … he's offered to cut the tree up for me."

Rose smiled. 'Oh good. You met Chase. What a sweetheart. He lives here all year round."

"That's what he said," Mena responded. "I think I remember his family from when I was younger and we came down here."

The woman nodded. "Oh yeah. The Harpers have been here for a pretty long time. That house might be one of the only ones that has never changed hands. That and your grandfather's. Most every other house here on the beach has been sold at least once since being built. People have been getting pretty good prices. Just a few miles down the beach, a developer came in and is building million dollar places. So the people that can't afford those are coming to Brandford to look for something more in their price range. Most of our families can't pass up those dollar signs when they see them, you know? But I've had more than a few stop back in here, regretting selling their homes. Because they found out they can't afford to start over and buy anywhere else. Everything is too expensive for those families that built here when it was nothing." She started putting the eggs and bacon into containers. "Have you decided what you're going to do with Christopher's place?"

Mena shook her head. "Not yet. I'm still just trying to get my footing in there. I don't know why I thought I could do it all in one weekend," she said with a smile. "It's a sweet place."

Rose nodded. "Yes it is. And your grandfather always had big plans for it. He'd come in here in the morning and tell me about what his next project was going to be. He'd sit over there," she pointed to one of the small tables along the windows that overlooked the beach, "and he'd say how he was drawing up the addition he was going to put on the back, or the new porch on the front. It was always something. He was a dreamer, that's for sure. But I think that made him happy. To dream about things like that."

Mena hesitated before asking, "Did he ever talk about selling his place?"

"Oh no. He said he'd never sell. Before he left last year he was saying that he was making plans to move down here permanently."

"Really?" It felt so odd to have this stranger know more about her grandfather than Mena did.

Again Rose nodded. "He only came down a few times between November and March. If the weather was okay. He said he didn't want to have to put heat in the house, but had finally made the decision to do it. I still can't believe he's gone. I'm just heartbroken."

"Thank you. I'm so glad he had people that cared about him,," Mena said softly.

The woman put the bags and coffee on the counter and Mena handed her the money to pay for what she knew would be a delicious breakfast.

"I'm sure I'll be back down at lunch time," Mena said with a little laugh.

"I'll be here. You enjoy that."

Mena held up the bags slightly. "I know I will. Thank you so much."

She once again sang quietly as she made the walk back to the cottage. When she turned onto her street she immediately saw that Chase was awake and ready to go. He came up over the small hill from the beach and gave her a wave.

"I have breakfast," she called out to him, smiling.

"Great! Let me just get a quick shower and I'll be right over," he hollered, jogging to his house and up the stairs.

Mena didn't want to, but she couldn't keep the thought out of her head: He looked even more handsome in the daylight.

She shook her head, having to laugh softly before going inside and getting two plates out of a cabinet and some silverware out of a drawer. She divided the food between the two plates and then put the cinnamon rolls onto a plate in the middle of the table. She finished her setting with one cup of coffee and one bottle of orange juice beside each plate. She didn't know how Chase took his coffee but she had milk and sugar ready to go if he needed either one.

It was only a few minutes before she heard him knock at the door.

"It's open," she called out, watching as the door opened slowly and he stuck his head in. "Come on in," she assured him. "You can leave the door open."

He walked in, moving toward the table where Mena was standing. "Smells delicious," he said. "Thanks for doing this. You sure didn't have to. But it's nice to have company at breakfast."

"It's the least I could do after how you spent your night helping me and my roof. Especially if you won't let me pay you." She motioned toward one of the chairs. "Please. Sit down."

"Thank you," he said as he pulled out the nearest plastic chair. "Were you able to get back to sleep?"

She nodded. "I was, surprisingly. I actually slept great. I feel really rested today." She started to sit down but then remembered to ask. "Do you need milk or sugar for your coffee?"

He shook his head. "Black is fine. Thanks."

Mena sat down, hearing the water lapping against the sand in the distance. "That sound never gets old, does it? What is it about water that is so soothing? I mean when it's not pelting you from the sky," she added with a little laugh.

He grinned. "It's a great sound."

"Were you in the water this morning?"

He nodded after taking a sip of coffee. "I try to get up and run every morning. When I'm done I just do a quick detour into the water to cool off."

"I never got into running. I'm one of those 'oh my ankle' kind of women as soon as I pick up my pace too much."

Chase laughed. "It's not for everybody." He took a forkful of the eggs and sighed. "These are delicious," he commented before adding a bit of bacon to the mix.

"They do a great job at the store. One thing I do remember from when I was young. Personally, I love to cook. But there's not really a lot here to work with."

"Living alone I do a lot more cooking than I'd like," Chase said, taking the lid off of his bottle of juice. "You never did say. How come you guys stopped coming?"

Mena decided to just shrug. "I don't really remember, exactly. I remember waking up to something going on one night and the next day, we went home." She shrugged again. She certainly didn't want to force him to divulge anything about his family that he didn't want known at this time, so she kept it vague. "And then when I got older, for some reason I was under the impression that my grandfather sold the place." She omitted the part where he straight up said he sold it. "I guess he was tired of us using it," she said with a little smile. "But when he passed, there was a letter for me. To please come here and take care of it for him. You know ... clean it up ... sell it ..."

"Oh man. You're gonna sell it?" Chase asked. "That's too bad. He loved this place. I mean your grandfather ... I never saw him without a smile on his face."

Mena nodded, eating a few forkfuls before asking, "Did my grandmother keep coming down here with him?"

"When are you talking about?" Chase asked.

Again Mena shrugged. "Nineties? Two thousands?"

Chase seemed to take some time to think about the answer, to catch that particular information from where it was tucked away in his brain. "I really can't remember the last time I saw Roberta."

"She passed away in 2005," Mena offered, as if that might help.

"I heard that. I'm sorry," Chase said sincerely. "But it was a few years before that. That I saw her down here, I mean. Man, I want to say like ... ninety-five maybe? And even then it wasn't every time."

"Really? But my grandfather kept coming down without her? Did he ever say why? That you remember?"

Chase was quiet for a moment. "Were you close to your grandfather?" he finally asked.

Mena shook her head, sadly. "We kind of drifted apart. He had some fight with my mother and ... it was made clear to me that I was a traitor if I continued a relationship with my grandfather. I'm ashamed to say that I just went with it. My family was starting to be all about drama and I just ... didn't want any part of it."

Chase nodded his head slightly as he continued to eat. "It should only take me a few hours to get the front cleaned up for you."

"I really do appreciate that. Please think about letting me pay you. I'm taking up so much of your time."

Chase smiled. "Actually it's Ron that should be paying me. It's his tree. I'll reach out to him this week and let him know." He looked across the table. "But if you feel obligated ... maybe we could do dinner tonight?"

Mena smiled. "That sounds nice. Thank you."

Chase nodded toward her left hand. "And just to be clear, I see the rings on your finger so I'm just ... being friendly. I don't want your husband to get the wrong idea."

"My husband ...," Mena said softly. "I don't think I'll be talking to him about having dinner or ... much of anything else this week. I'm here to take care of my grandfather's house but also to do some ... soul searching. Figure out where I'm going from here. I thought I could kill two birds with one stone. This place ... there's just so much to do. I mean if I sold it in the condition it's in ... I think I'd be giving it away. And my grandfather deserves better than that. Especially with how much you said it meant to him." She took a drink of juice. "At the store Rose was telling me about all of the plans he had for the cottage."

Chase's face lit up. "Oh yeah. He was going to raise it up so that he could really put some money into it. As it sits now, he didn't really want to sink too much into it in case it flooded in a storm. That's why he kept the cement floors and the drains." He looked around. "It's kind of weird, you know. Being here. It's exactly like it always was. Like he should walk in that door any second with his morning paper, cussing about the Phillies or politics or something."

Mena nodded. "Yeah, I haven't really done much. I swept up and dusted things off, but that's about it. I started going through his things but ..."

"Yeah, I get it. It's tough. Especially if you hadn't been in touch with him," Chase said softly.

"I think that's it. But I'm also finding things that ... I don't know. I'm just trying to figure his life out, you know?"

"Like what?" Chase asked gently.

She shook her head. "Nothing that I guess I want to get into right now. It's just ... some of it hurts my heart a little and ... hits too close to home. And I think I was really hoping to hear that all you'd seen was him and my grandmother so much in love and enjoying each moment together. I guess .... I wanted to believe in happily ever afters. I wanted to think that anything less than that was the exception to an otherwise beautiful rule. Which probably makes no sense. I'm sorry."

"Well, we just met ... again," Chase said with a little smile. "So maybe you'll feel more comfortable talking after we've spent some more time together. But I'm here to listen ... anytime."

"Thank you," Mena said with a sincere smile. "But what about you? You said you're over there alone ... where is your family?"

Chase hesitated before answering. "Well ... my grandfather passed back in the seventies and ... my dad just passed last year. He'd divorced my Mom, and she's remarried and living out in San Diego. My sister moved out there to be closer to her when she got married and was pregnant with her first kid. I guess she had the same relationship with my dad as you had with your grandfather. You listen to what somebody says and think that if you love 'em then you have to defend 'em. She defended my Mom."

"Against what?" Mena asked quietly.

Chase gave her a somewhat sad smile. "Maybe that's for another day too. Let's get to know each other before we scare the other one off with our family horror stories."

Mena laughed. "Deal." She put the last bit of egg in her mouth and then looked at the cinnamon rolls. "I think my eyes were bigger than my stomach. I was so hungry when I ordered our breakfast."

Chase's plate was clean and now he grinned, grabbing one of the rolls. "My eyes, however, are just the right size."

Again, the sound of Mena's laughter drifted softly around the cottage. It had been awhile since she had laughed at anything. It felt good.

"So tell me how I can help you with the clean up."

Waiting until he swallowed his rather large bite of the cinnamon roll, Chase answered, "Well, I'm going to cut up the tree. I have a wheelbarrow to take the pieces of wood next door and I'll pile them up behind Ron's house. Then I'll clean up the debris from your yard and we can just burn it if you want."

"Can you do that here? On a beach?"

He nodded. "I'll keep the hose handy, but it's only me and you on the street, so," he shrugged. "I think it'll be the quickest and easiest way. Then we can bag up whatever's left and put it in the trash."

"Is that what you do?" Mena asked.

"Well when I got old enough to kind of take over the house, I ripped out all of the growth and just put down rocks and brought the sand down. So I use some weed killer throughout the spring and summer and ... keeps it nice and tidy."

"Do you think I should do that here?"

"That's up to you. Christopher always wanted grass. Pissed him off that he could never get it to grow right. But no matter what he did, he always got those cacti coming up. You sure couldn't walk on it barefoot."

Mena just watched Chase as he talked about her grandfather. "What else did he want to do?" she asked softly.

"Well ... he wanted to take down that wall," he said, pointing to the wall behind the couch, " and put the kitchen back there, where the bedroom is. Have the back door go out of the kitchen. Put a deck back there. Then he was going to put a wall here. Right up to the side of the door and take that back. Have that area be the bedroom and bathroom."

Mena tried to picture her grandfather's design dreams and nodded. "That makes more sense than how it is now."

Chase nodded. "That's what he thought too." He got up from the table and walked to the doorway that now led to the bathroom. "So right here he was going to put a little alcove. Bathroom door to the left, bedroom door to the right. And then this space in front of me would be half bedroom closet and half linen closet."

Again Mena nodded. "And have the open area be front to back instead of side to side."

"Yes. He said that way you had the light coming from the front and back in the living area. He hated how dark it got in here sometimes." Chase looked around. "He had a drawing that he was always working on. He kept it ..." He walked over to the metal cabinets that had housed the candles. "May I?" he asked.

"Yes. Sure."

He pulled open the two doors and reached his hand up to the top shelf, feeling around. When he pulled his hand back out, he was holding a piece of paper. "Here it is," he said with a smile, handing it to Mena.

She took the paper and laid it on the table in front of her. It was a pencil sketch of everything that Chase had told her. She couldn't keep her eyes from pooling with tears when she saw her grandfather's handwriting. The same handwriting that had written her that note when he knew he was dying.

"Oh my gosh. I'm so sorry," Chase said quickly, seeing her tears. "Mena, I ... I didn't think. I'm sorry."

She tried to give him a smile but it was a poor attempt. "No, it's fine. It's just ... I lost so much time, Chase," she whispered. "You're talking about my grandfather. Telling me things that I should know." She shook her head.

"I've been so busy telling my husband what a terrible person he is, that ... I haven't taken the time to turn the mirror on myself ... Do you know what I mean? All this trip has done so far is to show me that I turned my back on a man that ... now ... I don't even know who he was. I'm finding cards, letters, ... coffee mugs for Pete's sake ... and it's like ... he's a stranger. And he shouldn't have been." She looked into Chase's brown eyes. "If I ask you a question, will you answer it honestly? Even if you think the answer might hurt me?"

"I wouldn't want to hurt you, Mena," Chase answered honestly.

"But ... would you anyway?"

"How about if you just ask and if I'm uncomfortable answering then I'll tell you."

She nodded. "Okay. I guess I can't really demand more than that. Thank you." She took a deep breath and let it out slowly, gathering her courage. "I think my grandfather was having an affair. I'm starting to think that might be what my Mom found out. And why my grandmother finally stopped coming down here."

Chase just looked at her, clearly uncomfortable. "That's ... not a question."

Mena smiled. "Right. Sorry. My question is ... you and your family have always been right across the street. Did any of you ever notice anybody else's cars here? Or did you guys see anybody that maybe you didn't recognize? Somebody my grandfather passed off as a friend or ... I don't know ... maybe he just came right out and said 'This is my girlfriend. She'll be staying over'."

Chase smiled.

"You seem relieved. What did you think I was going to ask?"

He just smiled again. "No, I never saw any strange cars on the street, and no he never introduced any strangers to me or my family as his girlfriend."

"Would you tell me if he had?"

Chase sighed. "Honestly, I don't know. But there were never any strangers coming and going. I promise you that." He clapped his hands together. "Now, I have to get to work. But why don't you just stay in here and relax. Breakfast was payment enough."

"You don't want my help?" Mena asked, pouting just a little.

Chase laughed. "It's your call. Just don't feel like you have to." He motioned toward the dishes on the table. "Can I help you clean up in here first?"

"Oh, no. Please," Mena said. "I will get this. And then I'll come out to see how I can help you."

Chase nodded. "Alright then." And, gracing her with yet another beautiful smile, he left the cottage and before long the sound of his chainsaw once again filled the room.

Mena went about cleaning up the dishes, but her mind was on 'Stevie'. "So if Stevie wasn't visiting you here ... what the hell was going on?" she whispered. Chase's family was there all summer, so surely they would have seen her. It wasn't like Christopher could bring her in the trunk of his car, in the middle of the night, and then forbid her to leave the cottage all summer. Maybe it was time for Mena to have a talk with her mother. To finally find out what happened all of those years ago. But as the sound of work being done outside drowned out her thoughts, she decided that talking to her mother could wait. As it had for so long.

Mena left the inside work behind and went outside to see if she could help Chase. She quickly saw that, even though it hadn't even been a half hour, the tree was almost completely cut up and stacked behind the neighbor's house. She also couldn't miss that the rest of the random, tall growth was missing as well. He was now raking what was left out from the front yard of the cottage, toward the road. He had removed his shirt, revealing more of his dark tan. She didn't think he spent much time behind a desk, that was for sure. His jeans were dirty and his feet were surely hot in the black work boots that he no doubt wore for protection.

"I come bearing gifts," Mena said, holding out a bottle of ice cold water.

He took it without hesitation, leaning his head back as he drank, emptying the bottle in one go. 'Thank you," he said.

"Chase, this looks amazing. How did you do it so fast?"

He gave her a smile, appreciating the comment as he wiped his face with a bandana that had been hanging out of one of the back pockets of his jeans. "Well I still have to finish up with the tree. But I was wondering, did you want to go with the grass? Or something more ... beachy?"

"I'd kind of like to honor my grandfather with the grass, but ... how would I do it?"

"We could lay sod down. Just put some soil or manure down on top of the sand and then lay the sod on top of that. Would cost a little bit, but it would make the place look really nice."

"Can I do that this time of year?"

Chase nodded. "Oh yeah. This is a good time. While it's still warm, getting some rain. It'll take root."

"Okay then ... yeah. I want to do that. I want to do sod. But I'm really not familiar with this area at all. Do you by any chance know who I could call to do that?"

"Yeah. I do construction so I have a company I call in to finish off the lawns when I'm done with a place. I can give them a call today if you'd like. See when they could take care of it." Chase paused. "How long were you planning on staying? I mean ... so I can let them know your schedule."

"I really didn't know. I had thought I'd just be here for a few days, but ... I can't stand here and say that right now I'm in a hurry to get back home," she said softly. "So I guess I can stay as long as I need to."

Chase gave her a smile as he nodded. "Good. Okay then I'll see when they can get over here. I'll stop what I'm doing then because they can clear this out in half the time it would take me. And no burning involved. If that's alright with you."

"Of course! I'm glad I can get you to stop working. So ... you're in construction? Is that why my grandfather talked to you so much about what he wanted to do with this place?"

He nodded again. "Some. But we were close. Friends. Like a second father. And he liked to talk. Most nights when I got home from work I'd stick my head in and check on him. Sometimes he'd say 'Oh Chase, tell me what you think about this new idea I had today'," he said with a somewhat sad smile. "And he'd have changed his drawing. A wall would be moved over six inches or a window would be bigger ..." He sighed. "I miss him. Him and my Dad." He put on a quick smile. "I'd say 'So Chris, are we gonna get started this weekend?' and he'd grumble and say that it wasn't perfect yet. It had to be perfect."

"What do you think he wasn't happy with yet?" Mena asked.

Chase shrugged. "I think it might have just been more fun to have that drawing to keep him busy," he said softly.

Mena's eyes widened. "Wait. You checked on him every day?"

"Most days, yeah. Why?"

"And you never saw another woman with him? He was always

alone?"

"I ... never saw another woman with him. I promise you. Your grandmother was it."

Mena studied his face for a moment and couldn't see any signs of deception. So the mystery continued. A thought came to her mind. "Of course, you work everyday, right? Maybe his girlfriend lived here at the beach. Maybe they visited during the day. Walked the beach together. Stuff like that."

Chase looked down at her. "How do you feel about all of this? You seem to want Christopher to have been seeing someone else."

"No, I really don't! I absolutely don't. There's just signs. Things I've stumbled across while I was cleaning. And I know I have to pack up the rest of his things and I'm scared of what else I'll find. I don't want him to ... be my husband," she said with a sad shrug.

"Your husband cheated on you?" Chase asked quietly.

Mena nodded. "With his secretary. The old cliche."

"I'm sorry."

"Thank you. He says it meant nothing, even though it went on for, I don't know, almost a year. How can that be nothing? But do I really want him to say he was in love with someone else? Or is the fact that somebody is just that much better than me in bed supposed to be the easier choice?" She looked up at Chase and her eyes widened. "Oh my gosh. I'm so sorry. I ... I can't believe I just said that to you. To anyone."

Chase gave her a gentle smile. "Well hey ... if it's okay for me to say ... I can't imagine that she's prettier than you," he said softly.

Mena could feel her cheeks burning. "That's so sweet. Thank you. Even if you're lying ... thank you!"

"I'm not and you're welcome," Chase answered. "You know what? Let me go call my friend and see what we can set up for the yard and then ... are you still up for dinner tonight?" he asked.

She nodded. "If you are. Did you want to eat here again or ..."

"No. Let me take you somewhere. If that's okay."

"Alright. Sure. But ... you have to keep it casual because I really didn't pack much."

Chase smiled. "I can do casual." He started to gather up his tools in the wheelbarrow to take them back across the street, but he stopped. "I'm sorry. If you only packed for the weekend ... I have a full laundry room in my house. So please feel free to use it if what you packed starts to run out," he said with a smile.

"That's so nice of you. Thank you. My mind hadn't gone there yet, but it would have ... in about two days," she said with a laugh. "What time do you want to meet up?"

"Is seven okay?" Chase asked.

Mena nodded, smiling. "Absolutely. That gives me plenty of time to uncover more uncomfortable family secrets. And Chase ... thank you again. For everything. I was ... so unprepared for this place and ... I don't know what I would have done if you weren't here. I probably would have run away screaming in the middle of the night."

Chase laughed. "You are very welcome. It's nice to have some company here. Even if it's just for a few days. I'll see you at seven."

"See you at seven."

Mena watched as he crossed the road with his tools and then went into his house. She turned around and took her phone out of the pocket of her shorts. She snapped a picture of the front of the cottage and sent it to Gemma with the message 'Handyman across the street helped with fallen tree from storm last night. Baby steps'

Gemma returned the message quickly. 'Not exactly the plaza. Decide what you're doing yet?'

Mena had returned to her place on the couch as she read the response. 'No. Might stay the week,' she sent.

'Just be careful and keep me posted. I love you'

Mena sent 'I love you too!' before putting her head back and closing her eyes. Images of Chase Harper immediately came into her mind, causing her to open her eyes back up quickly. She knew that her feelings of attraction to him were textbook responses to what she was dealing with at home. A man that she could dream would be everything that Tyler wasn't. But the reality was, feeling this way, Chase might as well have been her secretary.

"No," Mena said out loud as she stood up. "Because I would never act on it. I'm not you, Tyler. Or you, Christopher." It made her heart hurt to add her grandfather to the list but she was having trouble with it all. Maybe it was time to make that dreaded call. Mena walked over to the kitchen table and sat down, reluctantly dialing her mother.

"Wilhelmina?" was how Diana Weatherly answered the phone.

"Hi Mom. Did I catch you in the middle of anything?" Mena asked, secretly hoping the answer was 'yes'.

"No. I'm waiting for your father to get out of the shower. He played golf this morning and now we're going to be late for our movie."

Well it wasn't the 'yes', but at least it did put a time limit on the call. The next best thing.

"I'm sorry," Mena said before asking, "Do you have just a second to talk?"

"Of course. I'm always here for you. You're the one that doesn't seem to want to—"

"Mom, stop. Please. I just wanted to ask you about grandfather. About ... what happened all of those years ago."

"I don't know what you mean," Diana said matter of factly.

"You stopped talking to your parents. Our family stopped visiting them. You never said why," Mena tried again. "I just ... wanted to know."

"Well that doesn't seem to be a conversation we need to have now. They're gone. The past is the past."

Mena sighed. "That's really how you feel? It doesn't bother you? Did you see him before he passed?"

"Wilhelmina, you are a grown woman. If you wanted to see your grandparents, then you could have seen them. Don't blame all of that time you wasted, not seeing your family, on me. If anything, you just used me as an excuse to keep yourself from feeling guilty. It's not as if they're the only ones you ran away from ..."

Mena closed her eyes, wondering how she could have ever thought this would be a productive conversation. "Mom, I didn't run away ..."

"Let me ask you a question. What did my father's lawyer want with you?" Diana asked. But before Mena could answer, she said, "Your father's ready. We have to go. Talk later? You can tell me all about it."

Mena shook her head sadly, "Enjoy your movie," she said softly before hanging up and sitting her phone down. It was one thirty. The useless conversation had barely taken up ten minutes. There was still plenty of time to get some work done. Even without the answers she had been hoping to find.

She decided that she might as well open the bedroom door and start the job of packing up that room. She'd put it off because she was sure that was where she'd find the most of her grandfather's personal items. But knowing she'd be going out to dinner with Chase later, it didn't seem as bad.

A light, of sorts, at the end of what could be a tunnel of depressing discoveries. She pushed open the door, feeling the heat pour out against her. The room was dark, the shade at the window having been pulled down and curtains closed over top of it. She went over and pushed the curtains back, pulled up the shade, and then opened the window. Even though the air outside was warm, it was fresh air. Something the room desperately needed.

The full sized bed was made neatly, pushed up against one wall. The only other piece of furniture was an old dresser. On top of it was a lamp, a picture of Mena's grandparents, and a second photo that Mena had to walk over and pick up to see more clearly. She lifted the frame and smiled when she saw the cottage in the background. In the foreground was Christopher, Chase and another man that Mena didn't recognize. She smiled at the faces in the photo before looking over at the beautiful picture of her grandparents. Maybe she didn't know who Stevie was, but she knew that no man would have an affair that involved romantic looking cards and coffee mugs, and still have a photo of his wife out on display. In the bedroom no less. Maybe Mena had it wrong. Maybe Stevie just kept a lonely man company after the passing of his wife. Maybe Stevie just liked to send cards. Lots of cards. All of the time. Mena's head was swimming in unanswered possibilities.

A few hours later, Mena had Christopher's clothes bagged up, his personal belongings carefully packed, and the linens and curtains in a pile on the floor. Now, as she sat on the couch, she had on her lap a shoebox she'd found. The box was filled with photos. Photos that were obviously important to him. She went through them one by one. They spanned decades. There was a photo of a young Christopher and Roberta standing outside of the cottage. They looked so happy. There were photos of Mena and her siblings on the beach. And there were pictures of Christopher with some people Mena didn't know. Chase popped up in a few, and Roberta was in one or two. But for the most part it seemed to be a circle of friends that Christopher had made during his time staying at the beach. One man showed up in just about every photo in that group. A handsome man that reminded Mena of Chase. She wondered if it was one of his relatives. She left one picture out to take to dinner and ask him about it. She was starting to enjoy his stories as he helped her put together the pieces that made up the puzzle that was Christopher

D'Angelo's life.

CHAPTER FIVE

At seven o'clock sharp the knock came on Mena's door. She took one last look in the bathroom mirror before walking to the door and opening it. There stood Chase dressed in a pair of khakis and a light blue button up shirt with the sleeves rolled up.

"You are very prompt, sir," Mena said with a smile.

"Thank you. And you are ... very pretty,," Chase responded with a breathtaking smile of his own.

"Thank you very much." Mena had chosen a floral sundress for their dinner 'date'. She pulled her hair back from her face, but let the rest fall loose down her back. "Okay. I'm ready." She grabbed her bag from where it hung on the inside doorknob before walking out and locking the door.

"I'll drive if that's okay with you," Chase offered as they walked toward the road.

"Thank you. Except for walking to the store, I'm not too familiar with the area," Mena answered. "Where are we going? If you don't mind my asking"

"Not at all," Chase said as he opened the passenger side door of his truck.He waited until Mena had settled into the seat before he closed the door. When he was behind the wheel he answered the question. "I thought we could drive down to Reed Beach. They have a few good restaurants there and a boardwalk that's still open …"

Mena nodded. "Reed Beach, I remember that. We only went there once and got dinner. I wanted to stay there instead of here. I'm a little ashamed of that now."

"I think any kid would prefer a boardwalk to this quiet beach," Chase said as he drove them toward the main road that would eventually take them to the highway. "You don't appreciate quiet until you get a little older."

"True, but I just … I feel like I was kind of … I didn't appreciate much of anything. Like the fact that my family probably couldn't afford to stay anywhere else but here in that little cottage. When you're young your vision is so hyper focused on your own life. You just don't get that all of the 'old' people were kids once too. Do you know what I mean? As if the whole world started with whatever your first memory is."

"I never thought of it like that, but yeah … I understand what you're saying. Don't beat yourself up though. Did your family start going to a different beach when you stopped coming here?"

Mena shook her head. "I don't think my family ever went to the beach together after we were down here. The next time I remember going to the beach was going with a girlfriend after high school. And then we took my daughter later on …"

Chase glanced over at her as he drove. "A daughter?"

Mena nodded. "Tyler and I have one daughter. Gemma. She just started college this year. She doesn't like me being here alone. She wanted to come with me."

"You two are pretty close?"

"Very. I love her more than anything in the world. The one thing I took away from my relationship with my own mother was that I wanted to be … the exact opposite of how she turned out to be."

"I don't remember a lot about your mother but from the little bit I do, she seemed nice. Was that just something she put on in public?"

Mena shook her head. "No. That's just it. When I was young, she was great. I couldn't ask for a better mother. But it's like my family just … everything changed as we got older. Mom and Dad who had always seemed to be so much in love, changed to more of a … couple that tolerated each other. We stopped talking to my grandparents. My brother and sister just moved on, got married … We changed to one of those families that only gets together on the holidays. If that."

"I'm sorry," Chase said, his tone one of sincerity.

"Thank you," Mena said. "Don't get me wrong, it's not like I was abused or anything. It's just ... sad. Where we ended up. When I got married I was so glad that Tyler got a job offer in Connecticut. It was just far enough away, you know?" She looked over at Chase's profile. "What about you? Tell me about your family. You just have the one sister?"

Chase nodded. "Mom and Dad got their one boy and one girl and called it quits."

"But you spent a lot of time here growing up? Where did your family live?"

"I lived on the beach from June to September every year while I was young. For the other months, our house was in New Castle. Usually the family would come here the first weekend after school let out. Stay a week or two and then they'd come back a week or so before school started again. In between it was me, my sister and my grandparents. Then my grandmother passed when I was seven, and it was just the three of us."

"You liked being here?"

Chase nodded. "Oh yeah. Swam. Fished. Hiked. I loved it. I dreaded the summer being over."

"You loved it so much that you moved here permanently. Did you do that right after you got out of school?" Mena asked.

Chase shook his head. "By that time, my Dad owned the house and him and I lived here full time. And I ... never left."

"You said he passed not long ago?" Mena asked softly.

"In December," he answered.

"Was he sick? I mean ... I'm sorry. If you'd rather not talk about it ..."

"No. No it's okay. I think the doctors considered it natural causes. He was seventy-eight. Of course I hoped that he'd live a lot longer."

"You two were really close. You're so lucky to have had that relationship with him."

Chase nodded. "He was my best friend. Probably like you and your daughter. And to lose him and then Christopher ... I actually would sit on the deck and wonder if I could stay here without either one of them around."

"Thank you," Mena whispered.

"For what?" Chase asked, visibly confused.

"For loving my grandfather. Talking about him in almost the same way you talk about your father. The way that my family should have. I'll carry that guilt with me forever. The only thing that keeps me from collapsing under the weight of it is because he had you. And everybody tells me how happy he was."

"Don't get me wrong," Chase said. "I'm sure his life would have been better if he'd had you in it, but ...," he nodded. "Yeah. We kept him smiling as much as we could."

They drove along, leaving discussions of their pasts and families behind for now. Choosing instead to discuss the music on the radio, the homes they passed, and the perfect weather. Mena was finding it very easy to talk to Chase Harper. He was a friend that she hadn't even known how desperately she needed on this trip.

Chase had chosen a restaurant that offered dining on the boardwalk. They sat down, a cool breeze moving gently around them. Luckily Mena had thought to bring a little sweater that she now put on, enjoying their surroundings. The sky was still going through its magnificent display of the colors of sunset as they waited for their food, so it couldn't have been more perfect.

"So ...," Chase started. "Is the house doing what you wanted it to do? Keeping your thoughts off of your husband. His affair?"

Mena sighed. "I'm a multi-tasker," she answered with a little laugh. "I can feel guilt over my grandfather, think about how to honor him with what I do with his house, and also, still be able to feel the smothering sense of disbelief over Tyler's affair."

Chase smiled. "A lot of women would be crying every day. Getting hurt like that."

"Oh trust me. I had my share of tear filled days. You're seeing me later in the process," Mena said with a smile. "I have gone through the wide spectrum of emotions."

"Were you happy before that happened?"

Mena nodded. "Very. We had a really good life. Or ... that was my opinion. Which is why I wasn't sleeping with anyone else. It's funny how you have these moments that change everything. It's not the same as someone dying, but there is a little bit about it that's the same. Because it's like the Tyler that I dated and married ... he's not there anymore. The one that I talked to about everything ... I can't talk to him about this because of course his interest is covering his own behind. You know? This man that has his face and wears his clothes ... it's somebody different. But it's like I'm the only one that sees it. Which ... makes me sound crazy, right?" she laughed.

"Not at all," Chase answered quietly. "I can clearly see how it would feel like that. And if it were me, I'd probably want to think that they'd go back to being the person that I used to know."

Mena nodded. "But ... Tyler won't."

"What are you going to do?"

"I've spent weeks asking myself that very question. Gemma asks me. My friends ask me."

"Sorry—"

"No. No. I didn't mean it that way. I just mean that ... Do you know what hangs me up? The one thing?"

"You love him?" Chase asked.

"I do love him. But I don't trust him anymore. And I don't know how you can be with someone that you don't trust. What more is there? But ... no. I keep getting hung up on my vows. You know, standing before God and making the promise... til death do you part. Why get married at all if those words aren't going to mean something to you?"

"But he cheated on you. He broke his vows," Chase pointed out.

Mena nodded. "Yes. That's where my back and forth goes." She sighed. "I've known, realistically, for weeks that I can't stay with him. But this is the first time I've actually said it out loud to anyone, and honestly it makes me more than just a little sad. If I told anyone, it was like it would just make it real. Permanent. The reality that the life I thought I'd have forever is ... gone. And I don't want to see that hurt on my daughter's face. This affects more than just me."

Chase reached over and put his hand over Mena's, but quickly took it away. "I'm sorry," he said softly. "But ... maybe there's a new life waiting that will make you even happier."

She looked at him and smiled. "That's what I'm trying to focus on. What might be waiting, instead of putting so much thought into what I'm losing," she whispered. She realized she was becoming a depressing dinner companion so she changed the subject. "I found some pictures and I wanted to show you ... This man in them looks so much like you ..." She reached into her bag and pulled out the photo, putting it on the table between them.

Chase smiled as he picked it up. "That's my dad. Wow, look how young he looks."

"He was a very handsome man," Mena said. "It looks like him and my grandfather were close."

He nodded. "Best friends, I'd say. I'll have to show you some pictures I have sometime." He looked closely at the photo. "Look at those smiles."

Mena smiled. "I'm so glad that Christopher had your father's friendship. And ... that I have your's."

Chase smiled, handing the photo back to Mena. But any response he might have been ready to give was cut off by the delivery of their dinner to the table.

"How are you doing?" Gemma asked. "Is it helping? Being there?"

Mena was sitting on the beach, enjoying the morning sun, calmed by the sound of the water's movement. It seemed like the perfect time to check in with her daughter. "I'm doing okay," she answered after a slight pause. "I really am. I think I'm going to make the changes my grandfather wanted to make to the house. Chase and I had dinner last night and talked about it some more. So I'll probably be here a little longer than I'd planned initially."

"Are you sure you want to do that?"

"I am. I really am. I got it all cleaned up but ... hearing stories about how my grandfather's face would light up when he'd talk about making this place into his dream cottage just made me think that cleaning it up isn't enough. I owe him more than that. I want people to see his vision. If I sell it, I don't want people to walk in and think about how they could tear it down and put up something nice. I want them to fall in love with it and not want to change a thing."

"So this Chase guy ..."

"He's the one across the street. He spent a lot of time with Christopher. Was a good friend to him. More of a grandchild to him than I'd ever been."

"And he's cute?" Gemma pointed out. "And he took you to dinner?"

Mena laughed. "You're funny. Yes, he's very handsome but ... I'm married and ... friends do eat together. We spent almost the entire time talking about our families and the cottage." She sighed. "Sweetheart ... do you remember when I said that I didn't know what was going to happen with your father and me?"

"Yes."

"That wasn't one hundred percent truthful. I was just hoping that something would happen while we were apart to make me see things differently. That maybe I'd miss him so much that it would diminish the significance of what he'd done. How it made me feel. But it's kind of been the opposite. When I'm here it breaks it down to just black and white and ... I don't think we're going to ... fix this. I don't think I want to be in a marriage without trust. And ... I'm so sorry."

"Mom, you don't have to apologize. I could see how much pain you were in. And I knew that you were trying. Really trying. But that sadness ... it never left your eyes. And I don't want that for you. I want you to be happy."

"Thank you so much, sweetheart. And please know that if we do get a divorce that it's not a case of you having to choose sides. We're all adults and heaven knows your father is not the first married person to ever have an affair. It doesn't make him a horrible person. There's no reason for you to dislike him. It just makes him ... not the man I married. If that makes sense."

"It does, Mom. It really does. I mean, yeah, I hope that somehow we all work through this, but if not ... then ... I know we'll all be okay. Eventually." Gemma wanted to change the subject for her mother's benefit. "So tell me what's on the agenda for today. What are you taking on?"

"My goal for today is taking some of Christopher's things and donating them. I did some searching online and found a charity close by that hands out things to veterans. They also have a little store for the community. Everything my grandfather had down here is like new so I wanted to make sure it went somewhere that it would be appreciated. I couldn't think of anything better than this charity. Since he was a veteran himself."

"Mom, that sounds great! And you said the place is close by?"

"It seemed like maybe a half hour at the most. I have it all packed up and in the car so I'll probably head out soon. I'm also going to stop and get some bedding so that I can stop sleeping on the couch."

"Your back will thank you," Gemma responded. "I think it's good that you have all of this to keep you busy. It's a good reminder that you ... you can do anything you want. You don't need anybody else to make you happy. Like ... you've told me."

"You're a very smart woman," Mena laughed. "And thank you. I agree. The timing was pretty perfect. I think if I'd stayed home, your father and I would have said things we'd regret. Our interactions were coming from a place of pain and anger. Hopefully when I get back, we can just talk like two people that care about each other. Two people that ... just can't live together anymore."

"Do you want me to be there? When you do talk to him?"

"No, but thank you. You're still going to have two parents that love you more than the world. This talk will just be for him and I. Husband and wife," Mena sighed. "It's sad, though. I really thought we'd be together until we were old and gray."

"Well you would have been if it had been up to you," Gemma pointed out. "You didn't break up our family, Mom. Just because you're making this decision ... it's not your fault. I'm old enough to see things like they are. And if I was in your place ... I don't think I could stay either."

"Nobody better hurt my girl," Mena said, standing up and brushing the sand off of her pants with her free hand.

"And that's just how I feel," Gemma pointed out. "Nobody better hurt my Mom. Especially not my Dad."

"I'm glad we got to talk this morning. I love just hearing your voice. Talking to you, combined with the sound of the water ... it just really made me feel ... peaceful."

"I'm so glad, Mom. Please be careful finding that place. And be sure to take a picture of the bed when you have it made. I can't wait to see everything you're doing."

"You know I was thinking about that. If I do all of this work ... what if I kept the cottage for a year ... so that I could come back here next summer with you?" Mena suggested.

Gemma giggled. "I think that would be really cool. Oh Mom, I would really like that! If it's what you want to do."

"Unless I really mess things up, I do. I think it's what I want. It'll be nice to think of that while the work's being done. That all of the negative reasons that brought me down here ... It will all end up with you and I making happy memories. Like this place was suppose to be about. Like it was when I was young."

CHAPTER SIX

Mena pulled her car into the small gravel parking lot. Her mapping skills had been way off as it only took her fifteen minutes to get to the thrift store. She was almost disappointed as it was such a beautiful day for a drive. She parked the car and got out, deciding to go in first and make sure they accepted the items that were currently filling up her trunk and backseat. She slid her sunglasses up on top of her head to hold her hair back as she walked inside. A small bell announced her arrival from above the door.

"I'll be right there," a female voice called out from somewhere amidst the many racks and shelves.

"No hurry," Mena hollered back. She had started to look around when the owner of the voice popped up from the center of the room, making her way to Mena.

"Welcome," she said with a smile as she reached her customer. "My name is Elizabeth. Liz. I'm the owner of this little place. Can I help you find anything in particular?"

Mena couldn't help but return this woman's smile. It was infectious. And she immediately reminded Mena of Sarah. Something about her face made it seem as if they could be sisters. Liz was dressed in a plaid cotton shirt open over a tshirt, a tan pair of shorts, and black hightop sneakers that finished off the ensemble. Her blonde hair hung long down her back in a braid.

"Hi Liz. My name is Mena and I actually had some items to donate if you're accepting things today. I did some research and I liked how you're active with veterans so … I wanted to try you first."

Liz offered another smile as she nodded. "Absolutely I'm accepting donations. Always. Can I help you bring them in?"

"That would be great. Thank you."

Mena walked back outside, holding the door for Liz before going to her car and opening the full trunk.

"Oh wow. This is great! Doing some cleaning it looks like."

Mena took out one of the bags and handed it to Liz. "Actually my grandfather passed away and I've been going through his things."

"I'm so sorry," Liz said sincerely. "I see the Connecticut license plate so I'm guessing you're not from around here. Did your grandfather live in the area?"

Mena nodded. "Brandford Beach."

"Really? I spend a lot of time there. My family owns the Brandford Store."

"Are you serious?" Mena asked. "I'm in there at least three times a day since I got here. So maybe you knew my grandfather. Christopher D'Angelo?"

"Chris? Yes, I knew Chris. My aunt, who is usually behind the counter in the store, Rose, she just told me that he passed. Oh man, my heart just hurt so bad. What a great man! Always smiling. So you're the granddaughter that was given the beach house? It's so nice to meet you. Rose said that you were nice, just like Chris."

Liz picked up the bag and headed for the door, Mena following with two of her own.

Liz continued talking as she walked. "The Harpers would drive your grandfather to my store and I swear he would look at every single thing. Even if the piece had been here for months. And he'd never leave without buying something. I feel so honored to be the one to care for his things." She put the bag down by the counter once they were back inside, before she reached up and wiped a tear from her cheek. "I'm going to miss him," she said softly. "But it's so nice to meet you." She hesitated for a second before throwing her arms around Mena and giving her a tight hug. "It's like a part of

Chris is still here!"

Mena put her bags down and returned the hug. "Thank you for everything you said."

"Oh, just wait. I'll say so many more things," Liz answered with a laugh. "So tell me, are you going to be using the beach house? Chris loved that place."

"Apparently my grandfather told Chase Harper of the plans he had for the cottage. So I want to do them for him. Make it exactly how he dreamed it would be."

"Oh Chase. What a sweetheart that one is, right?" Liz said with a sigh. "He loved your grandfather as if it were his own second father. And why wouldn't he, right? I swear they were as much family as you could get. Even if it wasn't official."

Mena nodded slowly, but frowned just a little. "Were you ever at my grandfather's house?"

Liz shook her head. "No. I hung out with him at the store. He was always asking me to stop by ... I feel bad that I put it off for so long. Too long."

Mena saw the look of sincere sadness on Elizabeth's face and reached out to rub her arm. "Well it's not too late. You have a standing invitation to come visit as long as I'm here."

A smile immediately brightened up Liz's face. "Well maybe we can have Aunt Rose make us lunch one day and we can ... hang out."

Mena returned the smile. "That sounds perfect. You just let me know when."

"I guess before we do anything I should help you get the rest of the stuff out of your car. Am I right?"

The women laughed and talked while the never ending parade of bags and boxes were brought into the shop. When the car was finally emptied, Mena gave Liz her phone number and the cottage's address.

"The door is always open. I can't wait to show you Christopher's favorite place in the world," Mena said, giving Liz a hug. They said their goodbyes before Mena headed back out to her car and followed the directions to the closest Target store. She went directly to the bedding section, picking out a much more feminine sheet and comforter set than Christopher had on the bed previously. She also added two pillows to her cart before making her way to the clothing section and picking up a few more casual shirts, shorts and underwear.

When she returned to the cottage she had to laugh at taking in so many bags, after just taking so many out! She put the bags containing the clothing on the couch, taking the others to the bedroom. The window had remained open and the air felt so fresh. It made the room feel cozy instead of the stifling atmosphere it had when she'd first opened the door.

She sang softly to herself as she went about putting all the new items on the bed. She was smiling when she finished positioning the pillows against the headboard, the bed now fully made. She took a photo to send to Gemma before sitting down on the comforter, leaning back against the wall. She sent the picture with a text of 'It's making me tired. Can't wait for nighttime!', and then started scrolling through inspiration photos for the cottage makeover that eventually led down a Google rabbit hole.

She had no idea how much time had passed until she heard Chase's truck come down the street. With a million ideas now in her head, she hurried off the bed and out to greet her neighbor.

"I'm going to raise it," she said with a huge smile on her face, walking toward Chase's truck.

"Raise ... what?" he asked, a grin of his own playing on his lips. "Chickens? The roof?"

"Very funny," Mena said, continuing quickly. "The cottage. You said Christopher wanted to raise the house. That's why he didn't put in the good flooring or anything. So I want to raise it. I've been reading up on how they do it. I want it done. Don't you think that's a great idea?."

Chase couldn't help but laugh. "Okay. Okay. Calm down," he said, climbing out of his truck. "There's a lot involved with raising a house."

Mena nodded. "I know. But I was thinking that I'd hire you as my contractor and you could ..."

"Lift up your house?" Chase asked, still smiling.

"You've missed your calling as a comedian," Mena said. "You could oversee it. I figured I can't live in the house while they raise it so how about if they do it after I leave? You could make sure it got done right."

"After you ... ? When are you leaving?"

"It depends. Can we work on the inside first or would that be stupid?"

Chase looked into her eyes for a moment before answering, "We could work on the inside. I mean it's basically a square with a few walls. It might actually help to strengthen the place so that there are less chances for things to crack when it's being moved. Not that we'd want to put in the finishes or fixtures until it was raised."

Mena smiled. "Great!"

"So we'll put a hold on the landscaper and ..."

"Demolish the inside!" Mena said excitedly. "I mean ..." She stood by the pickup truck thoughtfully for a moment. "I guess I can't stay there if we're taking out the bathroom and everything. Well I'm betting that I could get a pretty good rate for a hotel room nearby. I saw some out on the main road. I can't imagine this is their busy season. And we can get started!" The words coming at a furious pace.

"Or you could ... stay at my place," Chase offered.."I have three empty bedrooms, so you'd have plenty of privacy and space. I mean, I understand if it would be better for your family to have you at a hotel, but ... you're more than welcome. I know we just met. Again. But it would cut down on the travel time back and forth."

Mena looked at the beautiful house, taking a moment to consider the offer before nodding. "Alright. Thank you. If you're sure it's no problem."

"I'll be gone all day and my bedroom is on the main floor. So you'd have the second floor all to yourself. We can store Chris' stuff in one of the other bedrooms if you want."

Mena nodded. "You're sure it wouldn't be an inconvenience to you? Positive?"

Chase shook his head. "Not at all."

"You're not at all positive?" Mena laughed.

Chase joined her laughter. "Not what I meant."

"I know. That was me trying to be funny too," she said with another laugh. "Seriously. Thank you so much." She didn't think before throwing her arms around her neighbor, giving him a hug. But she realized her mistake as soon as she'd done it, backing away awkwardly. "I'm so –"

"Please. You don't have to say anything," Chase assured her.

"I'm just ... very happy," she said quietly. "And I appreciate your help more than you know."

"It's fine. My pleasure."

"Okay. I'm going to go back inside," Mena said, pointing to the cottage as if she were part of a ZZ Top 80's music video. "and ... we'll make plans soon?"

Chase nodded. "Tomorrow after I get home from work? I can fix something for dinner?"

Mena nodded. "Thank you. That sounds good." Then she added quickly. "I'm sorry to keep you out here. Go. Go relax and I'll ... talk to you later." She turned quickly and made her way across the street. Once inside she leaned back against the door, her chest heaving with each breath. "Why did you do that?" she whispered. She peeked out the window and saw that Chase was still looking toward the cottage before turning slowly and making his way into his house.

That night Mena climbed in between the brand new sheets and settled in. For the first time in so long she wasn't consumed by the sadness of her marriage ending. Instead, she fell asleep with a smile on her face as she dreamed that her grandfather was still alive and was so happy that she was there with him, helping him do all the things he'd hoped to do.

"This is just how I was hoping it would all go," he said, giving her a warm embrace. "I love you Willie."

The words were still echoing in her mind when her eyes opened in the morning. She rolled over onto her back and looked at the ceiling. "I love you," she said, feeling as if his presence was still there.

Once she was showered and dressed, she started on her morning routine. The first thing being her stroll to the store. When she walked out onto the road, Chase was heading out to work. He stopped in front of the cottage.

"Good Morning," he said through the open passenger side window.

"I hope you have a good day," Mena responded, still unable to forget the awkward hug she'd forced upon him yesterday.

"Heading down for breakfast?"

She nodded. "My morning exercise," she answered with a smile.

"Then I guess offering you a ride would imply I don't care about your health?"

Mena laughed. "I'll still have my walk back," she said, opening the door and climbing into the passenger seat of the pickup truck. "Thank you."

"How did you sleep?" Chase asked as he put the truck in drive and pulled away.

"Really good. Better than I have in a long time," Mena said, watching the passing homes as they drove. She couldn't thank Chase enough for not making things uncomfortable between them. "You know what I want to do?"

"What's that? And yes, that question scares me now," he laughed

"I've noticed that most of these houses have little things in the yards or on the houses that have the family names. I want to get something for the cottage that says D'Angelo, or something like that. To honor Christopher."

Chase glanced over at her and smiled. "That sounds like a nice idea."

Mena nodded. "Something to always honor him." She looked over at Chase's profile. "How come you don't have anything like that? It looks like it's standard beach protocol."

He smiled without looking over. "Never really felt like advertising that I lived there," he said.

In no time they were at the intersection.

"I hope you have a good day at work. I can't wait to talk tonight. I just have so much in my head. So many thoughts and ideas," Mena said as she opened the truck door. "It's been a long time since I've been excited about anything like this. But it won't be like last night. I promise. I'll ... act mostly intelligent."

"I'm glad that it's all put a smile on your face," Chase said sincerely.

The smile was there on full display as Mena hopped down. "It really has." She closed the door and waved. "See you tonight."

Chase nodded and pulled away.

Mena crossed the road, making her way into the store.

"Good morning, Mena," was the immediate greeting she received from Rose.

"Good Morning, Rose!" Mena said in return.

"What will it be today?"

Mena made her way to the counter. "I met your niece yesterday. Liz."

Rose nodded. "Donating Chris' things I'm guessing?"

"Yes. It was hard until I started talking to Liz. Now I'm just happy that they'll be put to good use."

"She has a good heart. And loves her store so ... they're in good hands," Rose said. "I definitely think Chris would approve."

Mena smiled. "Thank you. I feel that way too."

Rose poured Mena a cup of coffee and put it on the counter in front of her. She was already pretty good at knowing what Mean wanted at any given time of day. The morning coffee was a given. "Was that Chase Harper that dropped you off?"

Mena nodded. "It was. He's going to help me with my grandfather's cottage. I'm really excited about bringing his drawings to life."

Rose couldn't help but smile. "That Chase ... he's a good guy. He's always helping me around here. Won't ever let me pay him. Not surprised that he's taken you under his wing too."

Mena sipped her coffee before saying, "He's a great guy. I can't believe he's not married. He's so sweet."

"And handsome. Right?" Rose laughed. "If you're into that."

"Handsome?"

"Well, I meant men. In general."

Mena laughed. "Oh. Yeah. So ... was he ever married?"

Rose shook her head. "No. Pretty much keeps to himself. The man works hard and then took care of his father and gave Chris any help that he needed. I can honestly say that I never saw him with a woman or ... a man. Anyone. Unless it was a man or woman that needed his help. Like the Victor family. He's an angel."

"That's really strange. A handsome, great, hardworking guy ... Not to mention a gorgeous house right on the beach. He's what you refer to as a great catch."

Rose smiled. "And are you ... casting your line into those waters?" Her eyes were twinkling with amusement.

"Me? No. No. Uh uh. I'm ... married. At least for now. I wouldn't ... No," Mena stammered.

Rose laughed. "Uh huh. Whatever you say. Okay so am I fixing you some eggs this morning?"

Mena could feel her cheeks blushing. It was last night all over again. "Yes. Thank you. I'm going to shut up now and just go pick out some fruit."

"Too late," Rose answered, still chuckling as she went to work on Mena's breakfast.

Mena picked out a bowl of diced fruit and took it back to the counter. Her mind was obviously still on Chase. It seemed like she couldn't shut herself up anymore if she tried. "But don't you think it's strange? A man like Chase ... never dating?"

"I didn't say he never dated. I don't know what he does when he's not here. He might be having the time of his life somewhere. But no real relationships. That's what I meant. And he deserves one. He's been through enough. He doesn't deserve—" Rose's sentence was cut off by the ringing of the store's phone. She reached to grab it while still tending to Mena's eggs. "Brandford Store," she answered.

Mena wandered away, giving Rose her privacy. But she couldn't help but wonder what Rose had been going to say. Chase seemed too relaxed and somewhat carefree to Mena. Other than the obvious pain of losing his father, he didn't give off the vibe of a man with a lot of baggage.

Branford was sure giving Mena more than just one mystery to solve.

CHAPTER SEVEN

Mena walked slowly across the street to Chase's house. In all the times she had been at Brandford Beach, as a child or as an adult, she had never been on this property. She had to admit that she was nervous as she walked up the wooden staircase to the door, knocking softly. As she stood there she could see inside, seeing Chase come into view, a smile on his face when he saw her.

"Right on time. Come in," he said as he opened the door.

All of the windows were opened allowing cool, fresh air to move inside of the house. The sound of the waves being brought in on each breeze. There was also something else, a delicious smell.

Mena closed her eyes and breathed in deeply. "Oh my gosh. Your house smells amazing."

Chase smiled as she now looked around. "Let's head out to the side deck. I'll show you what you're smelling."

Mena followed Chase through the beautiful, open living room and kitchen, through the open slider to the deck that faced the beach. "Look at this view," she sighed as soon as she stepped outside.

"I sit out here a lot at night. It's my favorite spot." He walked over to an impressive grill, raising the lid. "Looks like we have maybe five or ten minutes left on the steak."

Mena walked over to stand beside him. "Oh my gosh that looks as great as it smells."

He pointed as he said, "These are potatoes, and you can see the corn here. I also made a salad and have some wine. Would you like a glass while we wait? And talk?"

"That would be great. Thank you," Mena said, going to the railing and leaning her arms along the top as she looked out over the water. "I can see why you like it out here," she commented. "I think I'd be out here every day. The smells, the sounds, the view ... What more could a person want?"

He came up beside her holding out a glass of red wine. She took it, balancing it on the rail between both hands.

"It's pretty perfect," he said, "But I have to admit that it can get kind of lonely now that Dad and Chris are gone. I mean, you can imagine how it would be if you weren't here. And Rose will be leaving in a few days ... Sometimes it can be too much ... quiet for me to take."

Mena stood back up straight, taking a sip of the wine, facing her host. "What do you usually do? When there's not a neighbor asking you to cut up trees and raise houses? What do you do for fun?"

"Honestly?" Chase asked, going over to the grill to check the steak. "I enjoy my work. But when I'm not doing that, I'm actually ... writing."

"Writing? Like, a book?"

Chase chuckled. "As opposed to?"

"Well you could be writing a screenplay or ... I don't know. A book? Really?"

"That surprises you?"

Mena smiled as she looked at him. "A little bit. But I don't mean that in a bad way."

He nodded. "A bad way being that I don't look like I could string two sentences together, much less an entire book?"

"Right. That's not the way I meant it!" Mena answered. "But I think that's exciting. How long have you been interested in writing?"

"As long as I can remember, I guess," Chase said.

"How do you find the time? It seems like your work keeps you pretty busy. Not to mention ... demanding, needy neighbors."

He smiled before answering, "Nighttime usually is when I write. I'll sit out here with my laptop and just let it go ..."

"Oh wow. That is so very cool. Can I ask about what you're writing or ... do writers not want to talk about stories until they're finished? I don't know how that works," Mena said. "Don't creative types believe in jinxes and things like that?" she added with a smile.

"Honestly, I haven't met any other writers so I'm not sure," he answered with a little laugh. "For me, I really just have one story in my head that I wanted to get onto the proverbial page. Maybe I'll never show anyone. I don't know just yet. But ... it feels good to just go through this process."

"So me asking to read it ...?" Mena tried.

Chase laughed, shaking his head. "Sorry. It's nothing I'm even close to wanting to share just yet."

"Okay. I won't bother you about it. Just know that if you ever need someone to read it ... I'm your gal. Your person. Your ... reader."

"I appreciate it. Thank you. Hopefully," Chase said as he picked up a plate and put one of the steaks upon it, "when you come back in the spring it will be finished and I'll let you read it first."

Mena's eyes widened. "Really? Oh my gosh I would love that. Thank you so much."

"You realize that means you have to come back next year, right?" He added a potato and corn to the plate before placing it on the small round table.

"That is literally making my mouth water," Mena admitted, before adding, "Why wouldn't I be coming back?"

"Some people that lived three states away might just have somebody put a For Sale sign in the yard and call it a day," Chase pointed out as he made up his own plate. "You haven't said what your plans are once you get the place to match Chris's drawings."

He sat his plate on the table before pulling out Mena's chair.

"Oh, thank you," Mena said softly as she sat down. "Like you said, if I stayed in Connecticut I would be pretty far away to get the use out of the cottage that I'd want to, but ... honestly, who knows where I'll be living. Or how I'll be feeling." She shook her head. "I don't think I'll know until it's done and I think about somebody else staying in it."

"That's an honest enough answer," Chase said, with a shrug as he sat down.

"It's the kind of answer you deserve. But either way, I've already promised Gemma, my daughter, that we'd have one summer here at least, even if I decided to sell."

Chase took another drink from his wine glass. "Your family?"

"Yes. I mean, Gemma and me."

"Not your husband?" Chase asked.

"I try to picture that," Mena answered quietly. "But honestly, I just don't know. I ..." She shrugged sadly. "I can't imagine what would happen that would make me want that in my future. How he could fix the betrayal. Does that sound too dramatic?"

Chase shook his head. "Not at all. There's a lot involved in that decision. It's a heavy one."

Mena nodded, putting the first bit of steak in her mouth. She let out a moan of pleasure, smiling at her host. Once she swallowed she said, "Can I be completely honest with you and say that this is the best steak I have ever had? Hands down. From anywhere."

Chase smiled appreciatively. "Thank you very much. I'm glad you like it. I think I use that grill more than I use my stove inside. Even in the snow," he laughed.

Mena looked around. "Oh wow. You saying that ... I can't imagine what it's like when it snows down here."

"This will be my first winter without my Dad or Chris, and to be honest ... I'm not looking forward to it. I'm worried about feeling ... isolated. Suffocated."

Mena looked at the sadness in Chase's eyes as he spoke of his father. "I'm so sorry," she whispered. "If it helps you any ... being in a house with another person can sometimes be just as ... isolating."

He nodded. "Yeah ... I can imagine."

The rest of the meal was consumed around more enjoyable conversation of the hard and fast details of what was going to be done to Christopher's cottage. By the time the sky had transformed to the beautiful colors of nightfall, Mena had a pretty good understanding of what was going to be going on. Chase now had several pages of notes that he'd written out while they spoke.

"So tomorrow I will pack up everything else that's still in the house. The things I was going to keep," Mena said. She stood up, picking up her plate and glass. "Can I help you clean up?" she asked.

Chase grabbed his things and stood up as well. "I'll just put everything in the sink for now. They can go in the dishwasher later. How about if I take you upstairs so you can see the rooms? Let me know if you're okay with everything before we nail down the schedule."

She smiled and nodded. "Sure. Thank you. But I'm sure everything will be fine."

The two took everything in from outside. Leftover food was placed in the refrigerator and dishes into the sink before Chase took Mena upstairs. The second floor consisted of a short hallway with four doors. One to a hall bath, the other three opening to bedrooms.

Chase opened the first door on their left. "I thought you might like this one the best. Out the front you can keep an eye on Chris' place, and then out the side …" He walked over to a set of floor to ceiling curtains, pushing them open to show a set of French doors. "Look at this," he said, turning to look over his shoulder as Mena approached.

She stepped through the now open door and walked out onto the small balcony. She could see right over the water as the moonlight danced upon each small wave. "This is so beautiful," she whispered.

"So you think you'll be okay here while we work on the cottage?" Chase asked.

"Yes. Definitely," Mena said, nodding. "Thank you so much. And I promise I won't stay long. Just long enough to help out as much as I can. Before the real work starts."

"It's no problem. Honestly, it'll be kind of nice to have somebody else moving around in this house," Chase responded. "Unlike what you came here for. Peace and quiet."

Mena smiled. "From some things. But not complete solitude." She looked around the room, the minimal decor done in pale blues and tans. "Of course, there is one condition to me being here."

"Okay …"

"I pay rent and you have to let me help out around here. Roommates," Mena said.

"No rent is needed, but whatever else you want … ," Chase answered. "I want you to feel at home."

Mena nodded. "Thank you."

"I'll have the room freshened up for you tomorrow. So that it's ready when you are."

"Tomorrow or the day after. But I'll work fast. I promise."

"Take your time, " Chase answered sincerely.

That night Mena laid in her freshly made bed, looking at the ceiling as a cool breeze moved around the room from the open window. She had run away from her entire life, using her grandfather's wishes as the excuse she needed. But she knew it was all still there waiting for her upon her return. She couldn't keep her mind from going back in time to that morning when it all fell apart. ...

... Mena ran into the emergency room, terrified as she looked around for someone to help her find her husband. She was fighting hysterics and beginning to lose the battle. When she saw a nurse enter the waiting room she hurried over to her.

"My husband was in a car accident and was just brought in. Tyler Prescott," she said, her whole body trembling as she waited for an answer.

"Yes, Mrs. Prescott, your husband is in x-ray right now, but I will make sure someone comes out to get you as soon as he's back in his bed."

Mena nodded. "Could you just tell me if he's okay? The police officer didn't really say anything and I have no idea what happened ..."

The nurse gave her a reassuring smile. "They're doing all of the tests now and will have the answers to your questions very soon. But if it helps you, he was sitting up and talking before they took him to x-ray. I do know that much."

"Thank you," Mena whispered. That was something at least. "I'll just be right here then ... if somebody could give me news as soon as there is any."

The nurse nodded. "Of course. We have some vending machines right around the corner if you need anything."

The nurse continued on her way and Mena took a seat among the other apprehensive looking occupants of the ER waiting room. Tyler had left the house that morning like he always did. He even called on his way to work to remind her that he was taking her out for dinner that night. She hadn't given anything another thought as she'd then turned her attention to cleaning up the breakfast dishes, making their bed, and gathering up the laundry. But everything shattered when she answered her phone to find a police officer on the other end informing her that Tyler had been involved in a car accident and was being taken by ambulance to the hospital. There were no details. Nothing. Mena felt like she was in the middle of a bad dream as she ran around trying to find her keys. She looked everywhere except on the kitchen counter where they'd been all morning. When she finally saw them and got into the car it was a miracle that she made it to the hospital in one piece. Between her tears and her need to get there quickly she was sure she hadn't made the safest driving decisions on her way.

Now she sat in the waiting room praying quietly that Tyler would be alright. She jumped out of her seat when a nurse approached.

"How is he?" she asked quickly. "Can I see him now?"

The nurse smiled sympathetically. "I'm sorry. He's still in x-ray. But I wanted to give you his things for safe keeping." She held out a plastic bag. "I'll let you know as soon as you can see him."

Mena took the bag and returned to her seat, fighting a new wave of tears. She had been with Tyler for twenty years and she just couldn't imagine going through a single day without him. He had to be okay! She opened the bag and looked at the things inside. The shoes that he'd sat on the bed that morning and put on. His wedding ring, watch, his wallet, and his phone. She sighed sadly, holding the bag on her lap, hoping for time to pass more quickly. The light from Tyler's phone got her attention. The screen lit up with an incoming message. She reached into the bag and pulled it out, the screen still on, letting her see that he had fifteen new messages. It was only then that she realized that his office was probably wondering where he was. So she opened his phone in hopes that one of the messages would be from his partner or a co-worker and she could let them know what had happened. She opened up the list of unread messages and frowned slightly when she saw that twelve of them were from someone named Nick. But among the other messages was one from Sam Wilcox, Tyler's friend and partner. She quickly typed a message.'Hi Sam. This is Mena. He's been in a car accident and I am at the hospital with him.'

The response she received was almost immediate. 'Mena, I am so sorry!!! How is he? Do you want me to come there? Is there anything either of you need? Anything I can do? Please call when you can.'

She responded with 'Thank you. He's getting tests. I'll call when I know more' before turning her attention to Nick. Obviously this was someone desperate to get ahold of Tyler, so she thought she should reach out to them as well. But when she opened the most recent message she felt as if her heart had stopped beating. The nightmare feeling had returned. The message was just the latest in an ongoing conversation between this person and Tyler.

'Baby I'm losing my mind. Please text me back or call. What happened?? I've tried to call you back but there's no answer. I'm so close to calling your wife. That's how scared I am. I love you so much!!'

Mena scrolled back further, passed the morning's frantic pleas, begging Tyler to respond. Finally she found the last text from Tyler, timestamped the night before at 11:13. It read 'Goodnight Nikki my love. I'll be dreaming about you! I'll call in the morning'

Mena started breathing heavily, as if the air might not come if she didn't force it. At 11:13 the night before she had been lying beside Tyler in bed while he claimed to be returning work texts. Before putting his phone down and making love to her.

Tears rolled down Mena's cheeks, but now they weren't because of the accident. They weren't because of her fear. They were for her marriage. Her hand was shaking as she put her finger over the phone icon on the 'Nick' message thread. The call was answered before it even rang one full time.

"Oh my gosh Ty, thank God! I have been so worried. What happened? One second you were there and the next you were gone!" a woman's frantic voice gushed. When there was no reply she said, "Ty? Baby, are you there?"

Mena swallowed hard before whispering, "This isn't Tyler. It's his wife."

Now it was Nikki's turn to go silent.

"I'm at the hospital, waiting for word on my husband's condition because he was in an accident. Apparently when he was talking to you, so ... he doesn't have his phone now. I do," Mena continued to whisper, her voice shaking.

Mena could hear the woman on the other end start to cry.

"Mrs. Prescott ... please tell me what happened," Nikki finally said.

Mena cut her off. "Please don't," she whispered. "If my husband wants to call you if and when he's able, I'm sure he will." And she disconnected the call.

She wanted to run screaming from the emergency room. Run in the morning sun until she woke up from this horrible dream. She wanted to see Tyler laugh when she told him about the alleged affair she dreamed he was having. About how she only found out after he'd been in an awful car accident. She wanted to be able to throw her arms around him and make him promise that he'd never be unfaithful. She wanted to hear him swear that he never would and tell her that she was being silly for even entertaining that thought for the briefest second.

She wanted him to mean it.

Thankfully, after some time, she started feeling numb. The gut wrenching pain had somehow morphed into a horrible nothingness. She'd allowed herself to cry. Afterall, it was the emergency room. Nobody would think twice about tears in a hospital. But eventually the tears stopped and she wanted to just curl up and sleep until it was over. Until she was sure the pain wouldn't return. If that was ever to happen. She resisted the urge to read the complete text list on Tyler's phone. It was now tucked back into the plastic bag. She knew what she needed to know. No need to torture herself.

She considered leaving, but lost her chance when that same nurse came out with a smile on her face.

"Mrs. Prescott? You can see your husband now."

Mena forced her legs to support her as she stood up.

"You can follow me," the nurse said.

She made small talk along the way, but Mena barely heard a word. All she could think about was seeing Tyler's face. Her emotions were a painful roller coaster and she wasn't sure if there was another drop coming. It was like the all too popular horror movie trope where you think the horror has passed, only to have at least one more jump scare before the credits rolled. She felt physically ill when the nurse informed her that they'd reached Tyler's room.

"If either of you need anything, just let me know." She gave Mena a smile before continuing on down the hall.

Mena stood outside the door, gathering her strength before pushing it open. The lights were off in the room and Tyler was lying in bed. There was a bandage on his forehead and his left arm was in a cast. His eyes were closed and it appeared that he was sleeping. Mena walked in quietly and took a seat in a chair near the end of the bed. She kept her eyes off of her husband, choosing instead to look out the window. But too soon she heard his voice.

"Hey baby," he whispered.

Mena couldn't force her eyes to move to his face. So instead she continued to look out the window as she responded with a softly spoken, "Hey."

"Sorry about all of this. For worrying you," he then said. "I can't even remember what happened, really. They said it's probably because of hitting my head."

Mena nodded slowly, tears springing to her eyes. It was the voice of her beloved husband. But it was all just a mirage. The man she'd known was gone. Wiped out by a phone call. Killed in a traffic accident.

"Baby?" Tyler whispered. "Are you okay? I'm sorry if I scared you. They said I'll be fine. Just a little recovery, but nothing permanent. It'll be okay."

Finally she turned her head to face him.

"Aw, baby," he said softly. "Come here. Come over here." Reaching his right hand out to her.

All she could do was shake her head.

"Why?" Tyler asked. "Come on. Talk to me. It's okay. I'll be home in no time. I promise. Oh sweetheart. I'm so sorry."

She opened her mouth, not sure that the words would come, but they did. "For what, Tyler? Tell me exactly what you're sorry for. Please," she whispered.

"For upsetting you. For scaring you."

She watched his face. "Is that all?"

He was quiet, clearly not understanding. Or pretending not to. She couldn't be sure which.

She stood up. "I'm glad you're going to be okay. I really am. But I'd better go. Gemma is going to be home soon and I don't want her to worry. Do you want me to take your things home?" she asked, holding up his bag.

"Yeah. Okay," he said softly. "Mena, what's wrong?"

"Like you said, Ty, I was just scared. I guess I need to let everything sink in. Process it all."

He nodded slightly. "Will you come back tonight?"

"I'll see," she answered. "I'm glad you're alright." She headed for the door, leaving a confused Tyler watching after her. With her hand on the doorknob she turned to look back at him. "Oh, you probably want your phone …" She reached into the bag and pulled his cell phone out, walking back to the small table by his bed. She laid it down gently, her hand still on it as she said, "You probably want to call Nick."

She didn't miss the look of fear that he tried to hide as quickly as it came.

Mena nodded before turning again, and leaving the room. As she walked to her car she wondered if Tyler was already on the phone with his beloved Nikki. If he was being told that Mena had spoken to her. She wondered if her husband was now maybe feeling even the tiniest bit of the pain and fear that Mena had felt.

CHAPTER EIGHT

The next day the sun rose over the water, fighting to break through a layer of clouds that had gathered overnight. Mena got up, showered, and got herself a cup of coffee. She pulled her hair back and started the job of boxing up yet more belongings. At least this time there wasn't a complete house to pack. But there was enough work to keep her mind off of last night's dreams. She sealed every box that had Christopher's things in them, and then left the one open that had her own toiletries, groceries, etc inside. By the time noon came around, the only things left to do were to take out the bed, dresser, couch, chairs and tables. The boxes and lamps were on the front porch. With several hours left before Chase got back home, Mena decided to take a drive to visit Liz. When she arrived there were only a few other cars in the parking lot so she took the spot near the door and walked inside.

Liz immediately looked up, breaking into a smile. "Mena! Nice to see you back!" She walked from where she had been unloading a box to the front of the store. "Are you looking for something or just in the neighborhood?"

Mena returned the smile. "I had some time to kill so I thought I'd see if you got anything new in. And just check in with you."

It appeared that there were three other shoppers in the store, but Liz gave her complete attention to her new friend.

"Want a cup of coffee?" Liz asked.

"I can never have too much coffee. That would be wonderful. Thank you."

"Be right back."

Liz disappeared to the back of the store while Mena browsed through the items near the front counter. She recognized some of Christopher's things and it made her smile. She was proud to have his belongings on display at this beautiful store. She was admiring a necklace when Liz returned.

"Here you go," she said, holding out a coffee mug, steam rising from the dark liquid.

"Thank you," Mena said, taking the cup between her hands. "I just love everything you have here."

"Thank you. The community is pretty generous, I have to admit." She pulled a wooden chair over. "Please, sit down. How are you doing? How is the house coming? I know it's just been a few days but have you gotten anything done?"

Mena nodded. "Yeah. I mean, the plans are going well. I'm going to make Christopher's dreams come to life with it. The cottage. I've hired Chase to oversee it. We're going to have it raised, like my grandfather wanted, and then redo the inside to match his drawings."

"And then ... sell it?" Liz asked.

Mena was quiet for a moment as she looked out the front window at the gray sky. Images of her home, her family, and the cottage all going through her head at the same time. When she finally answered it was only to say, "I'm not sure."

"Well if you want my opinion, I'm not sure what you look like when you're at home, but right here, right now, I see a pretty content woman. Beach life certainly suits you."

Mena couldn't help but smile slightly. Appreciating Liz's comment. "Is that how I look? Content?"

"Aren't you? Did I get it wrong?"

"Well ... let's just say that my real life ... my non-cottage life at home, with my husband, is kind of a wreck," she said softly. "He had an affair ..."

"Oh shit. I'm so sorry," Liz responded sincerely.

"Thank you. It's okay, it's just that ever since I found out ... I just felt like 'our' life was 'my' life, and 'my' life was over. That probably makes no sense, but I've been so wrapped up in the fact that what he did ruined the life we had built, that I never even considered that I'm ... me. And this 'me' is enjoying having this cottage to kind of wrap around myself. It's a pretend new life, but I'm still enjoying this little bubble. Safe from the reality waiting for me at home.." Mena couldn't help but laugh just a little. "I'm so sorry for talking about all of this. I mean you've met me once and now I'm treating you like you're my therapist. It's just that you remind me so much of my best friend that I feel ... comfortable talking to you. Too comfortable, I'm sure."

Liz laughed. "You can talk about anything you want. That's what sharing a cup of coffee is all about. And you, Mena, are stretching your wings. Feeling that solid ground beneath your feet. Without a cheating husband by your side. I think that's what I'm seeing."

"You don't see a desperate woman, hiding from her life? Mena asked.

"I don't see desperation in you at all, girl. But don't make it all about one or the other. You can still be hurting, but you're also healing. That's what beach life lets you do. And it gives you strength. And strength is always a good thing. Because decisions you make when you're feeling strong ... Those are the right decisions!"

Mena couldn't help herself. She put the coffee mug down and reached over to give Liz a tight hug. "Christopher has no idea what he did for me," she said before letting go. "Giving me the chance to meet the great people in his life."

"Or maybe he did," Liz said softly, reaching over and patting Mena's arm. "Did he know about what your husband did?"

Mena thought about that question, wondering if there had been any way her grandfather would have known what Tyler had done. She hadn't told anyone in her family. Gemma and a few close friends knew. That was it.

"I don't know how he would have known," she finally answered.

"Well he was a special old guy. Maybe he had his ways!"

Mena thought back to Christopher's letter. "Is that what he was telling me?" she whispered.

"What's that?" Liz asked before sipping her coffee.

"Oh ... nothing. It's nothing."

The two women visited for almost an hour more before Mena

figured she should get back to the cottage and let Liz get back to work. With a hug for her new friend, and a sincere thanks for the visit, Mena was on her way again.

The skies looked like they may give way to some rain, so when Mena got back to the cottage, the first thing she did was take everything back off of the porch and into the house again. She had just finished when she heard the first rain drops fall.

The unexpected afternoon of showers brought Chase home a little earlier than he would have been had the sun kept control of the late autumn sky. Mena was out on the porch, giving him a wave when he stepped out of his truck. He put his head down and hurried across the road, coming to stand beside her under the cover of the porch roof.

"The weather man did not say it was going to rain this afternoon," he said, his dark hair dripping beads of water onto the concrete floor.

"I know. Which is why I had everything out here this afternoon. And then took it all back in," Mena laughed. "Twice the workout."

Chase smiled. "You already have everything packed up?"

Mena nodded. "I didn't fool around today. I was on fast speed."

"Well then ... do you want to just take your own stuff over tonight at least? Since you don't have your sheets or anything out. And maybe it would actually be good to get yourself settled before bringing everything else over and starting the renovation."

Mena was quiet for a moment before asking, "Are you sure? You wouldn't mind?"

"Not at all," Chase answered. "Do you want to show me what stuff is yours and I'll grab it? So you can close this place up for the night?"

Mena nodded, turning to go into the living room, but she stopped. "You're positive?"

Chase laughed. "Go!"

She smiled. "Okay. Thank you. Right this way."

He followed her inside where she pointed out the box that had her own things inside. She went around and turned off the lights and closed the windows that faced the opposite direction of the rain that had provided her with sweet smelling fresh air during the storm. Then she grabbed her suitcase and her bag and motioned toward the door.

"After you, sir," she said.

"Ready to make a run for it?" Chase asked when they were both once again on the porch, the door locked behind them.

"Ready as I'll ever be," Mena said.

"Okay. Here we go!"

Chase opened the porch door and held it for Mena before they both took off across the street as fast as they safely could. The last thing either of them wanted was to slip and end up spread eagle in the middle of the road. Mena's things strewn all around them. Once they were both safely inside they sat their respective things down on the floor and sighed.

"I'm soaked!" Mena laughed.

"Me too! Straight through." Chase put her box down before saying, "There are fresh towels in the bathroom upstairs if you want to dry off or change or … whatever."

"Thanks. I think I will. Before I warp your floor." She picked her suitcase up again and went up the stairs to the bedroom Chase had pointed out the last time she had been in his home. She immediately kicked off her shoes before putting her suitcase down in a nearby chair and opening it up. She took out a dry t-shirt and pair of pants and then walked to the bathroom. She started off by using a towel to dry off her hair and her face, and then changed into the dry clothes. Once she felt she was presentable again she made her way back downstairs.

Chase was no longer in the living room, so she kept herself occupied by looking at the photos that were sitting around on tables and shelves, and those that were hung up on the walls. She smiled at pictures of Chase and the man she now knew to be his father. When she moved to the kitchen she leaned closer to the refrigerator to see a picture that was held by a magnet to its door. She gently removed it and smiled as she saw Christopher's face. He was on one side of Chase's father, while Chase was on the other side. She was still looking at the photo when Chase came out of his bedroom, in dry clothes, his wet hair combed back from his face. Unheard by Mena.

"Are you hungry?" he asked.

She jumped, dropping the photo to the floor. "Oh my gosh. Sorry. I didn't hear you come in. I guess I was snooping." She bent over to pick up the photo that had landed face down.

"I'll get it," Chase said quickly, but Mena already had it in her hand.

She started to hand it back to him, but saw the wording on the back of the photo, in Christopher's handwriting: "Chase, Stevie, and Me. 4th of July 2020".   She turned slowly toward Chase, asking softly,   "Your father's name is ... Stevie?"

Chase nodded. "Steven, but yeah. Some people called him Stevie. His friends."

"So the things I found ... Your father and my grandfather ....?"   She wasn't even sure what she was asking. It seemed ridiculous. Christopher D'Angelo was happily married to Roberta until her death. Too many thoughts were swirling around Mena's mind to make sense of any of them.

Chase watched her face. Waiting for her question to form completely before he answered.

"What does this mean? Were they ... ? The cards ....? The mug ...? Your father? Stevie? Was he ...?" Mena stammered.

Chase nodded. "In love with Chris? Yes," he whispered.

Her eyes widened. "But ... how could you have not said anything? I asked ... Practically since the first time I saw you. But you just let me go on and on ..."

He shook his head. "You asked if I'd seen Chris with any strange women. I answered you truthfully."

"You were playing with words," Mena said.

Again Chase shook his head. "I listened to your questions very carefully and answered them honestly." He leaned back against the kitchen island. "Mena, I have lived here in this house most of my life. My priority from early on was very focused. Taking care of my dad. Protecting him. From my own family. From strangers. And when he started having feelings for Chris, then I protected him too. They were from a different time and weren't comfortable in public. So I was there for them. And when you showed up ... I didn't know you. I didn't know your feelings about anything. All I knew was that you seemed to have very black and white feelings about relationships."

Mena's eyes widened. "Black and white? You think I would have cared if my grandfather was gay? Or bi? Or ... whatever you're saying he was?" she asked.

Chase shrugged. "Look, I liked you. And if you did have a problem with it ... I guess I really didn't want to know just yet. I wanted us to know each other better before having this conversation. But ... I never lied to you,

Mena. That's not who I am."

"But ... my grandmother," Mena whispered. "I didn't want my grandfather to have cheated on her like Tyler cheated on me. I wanted him to be better than that. Kinder."

"He was. She knew," Chase said. He was quiet as he let that knowledge settle in Mena's head before adding, "Apparently she'd known since before they were married. Chris said that back then there was no chance he'd have been able to live openly with a man, and he loved Roberta with all of his heart. And she loved him. So, being one hundred percent honest with each other, they made the decision to get married and have a life together. She was an amazing woman. She's the one that told him to say he'd sold the place. When she saw that my dad and Chris had feelings for each other ... she didn't want to rob Chris of that chance. Now that he finally had it. To live an authentic life. For the first time. She wanted Brandford to be his safe place. So she gave that to him, and she stayed in the position of his very best friend until she passed."

Mena just looked at Chase's face for a moment before quietly saying, "I wish you'd told me."

"They might not be here anymore, but I can't just stop feeling protective of them. People have made me that way. It can get pretty ugly," Chase whispered. "I'm sorry."

Tears came to Mena's eyes as she nodded. "I understand. I do. And ... thank you."

"For what?"

"For loving Christopher this much." She wondered how many times she'd say that to Chase.

"He was like my second father. Other than my father ... he was the only family I had." He sighed. "Can you forgive me for not telling you all of this days ago?"

Mena nodded. "You saw a woman that was freaking out thinking her grandfather was unfaithful. Let's add gay to the mix so that she can feel even worse for her poor unsuspecting grandmother," she said with a little smile. "I get it. But please ... I know you didn't lie but ... we're dancing really close to semantics. So if there are any other family secrets, do you think you could tell me now?"

"I promise you that if Chris had any other secrets from you, I don't know anything about them," Chase said.

She gave her host a smile, wiping her cheeks. "You promise?" she asked softly, extending her hand.

Chase smiled as he shook her much smaller hand. "No more secrets."

CHAPTER NINE

With the rain beating against the windows, Mena and Chase sat in the living room. Mena held a glass of wine in her hand but words had temporarily escaped her. Instead she was inside of her own head. Replaying those family memories that now had the vibrant coloring of new information.

Of truth.

"How about if I put on some music?" Chase suggested, breaking the silence. "My father has quite a vinyl collection that spans decades. I think he was more proud of his records than he was of me."

Mena broke herself from her thoughts and did her best to smile. "I love music. Sure."

"Anything you truly hate?"

The next smile came a little easier as Mena answered, "Very little."

Chase got up from his seat and walked over to the shelves that held his father's precious collection. Rows of albums that had been played so often, lined up alphabetically.

"Doesn't really seem like a Grand Funk kind of night," Chase said as he ran his finger along the edges of the albums, reading the titles. "Are you a Tom Petty fan?" he asked, looking over his shoulder.

"With or without his Heartbreakers?" Mena asked.

"With."

"Trick question," Mena said with another little smile. "I like him either way."

"Okay then." Chase took an album out of its place on the shelf and carefully removed the record, placing it gently on the turntable. Soon 'I Need To Know' filled the room.

"Nice," Mena sighed. She looked over at Chase as he sat back down. "Tell me about when they met?"

"Really?" he asked softly.

She nodded.

"Well, they'd known each other for years. Casually. Because, you know Dad would come stay at the house a few times during the summer. But it wasn't long after my grandfather died that my Mom filed for divorce. She got the house that we had lived in year round, so my dad moved in down here full time. I asked if I could live with him and my Mom really ... didn't care. So I moved in here too."

"How could a mother not want her child with her?" Mena asked softly.

Chase shrugged. "Well, I think my Mom had her suspicions about my dad. Even I knew something was ... I don't want to say 'off' with my Dad, because that would sound like I thought something was wrong with him. But ... he was different. In all of the best ways. In my opinion at least. He felt things differently from most of the other people I knew. He appreciated colors ... not just the sunsets. I mean everybody loves them. Just ... anything. When it would rain he would walk outside and close his eyes. I'd stand beside him and he'd say 'Close your eyes, Chase. Just listen'. He found joy ... beauty ... in every single little thing. And he was kind," Chase's voice broke just a little bit. "He was so kind," he whispered.

"He sounds like a really wonderful man," Mena remarked softly.

"My mother would think she was insulting me when she'd holler 'you're just like your father'. Man, to me that was the biggest compliment I could ever get. My dad was my superman. If we were in the store or something and I even thought somebody looked at him wrong ... I was ready to fight."

"Did people look at him ... wrong?" Mena asked.

"It wasn't until my grandfather passed and my dad and I started doing most things together. Just the two of us. That was when I started seeing things a little more clearly. My dad was ... soft. Like a true flower child, you know? He never put an unkind vibe out into the world. And if people said something under their breath about him when they passed us in the juice aisle at the store ... They'd never get a reaction out of him. He'd hold me back when I got around fifteen or sixteen. Big enough to want to stand up for him. You know? Like 'nobody whispers about my father' or 'nobody better roll their eyes at my father' ... He'd just give me this beautiful smile ... He had a dimple on his right cheek ... and he'd say 'don't ever let anyone force you to stoop to their level. You always have the power to choose to be the better person'," Chase shrugged slightly. But he noticed then that Mena's glass was empty. "Some more wine?" he asked.

"That would be nice. Thank you."

He stood up and took her glass, walking to the kitchen where he poured some more wine for both of them. Mena watched, hearing him starting to sing along with the next song on the album.

'You think you're gonna take her away, with your money and your cocaine. You keep thinking that her mind is gonna change, but I know everything is okay. She's gonna listen to her heart ...'

"Maybe instead of a writer, you should think about a future as a singer," Mena said with a smile.

He turned around, a glass in each hand as he walked back over to her. "Of course that was my first dream. Isn't it everyone's? To be a rock star?" he said with a little laugh.

Mena took one of the glasses from him. "So your father was really into music?"

Chase nodded, sitting back down, "He loved music. He played guitar. Always had music playing. I'm surprised this turntable still works. It has definitely been worked hard over the years."

"I like this song."

"Yeah, me too. Dad was a big Tom Petty fan. Saw him a few times when he was still playing clubs. I used to love just listening to his stories."

"Did my grandfather enjoy listening to music with him?"

"Oh. I'm so sorry."

"For what?"

"You asked me to tell you how they kind of ... met. And I've been all over the place."

"No. Not at all. I'm enjoying hearing you talk about your father. I like getting to know him through your stories," Mena said sincerely. "I wish I could remember him."

"You didn't even remember me," Chase said with a smile.

"I was in my own world when we'd come down here. It's no reflection on you. I promise."

"If you say so." Chase took a deep breath and let it out slowly before continuing. "I don't really talk to too many people about my dad and Chris. As you can probably guess by how much I'm rambling tonight," he said. "But as for them getting together, I think it was maybe a year or so after your family stopped coming down. Kind of ironic really. Or ... deja vu?"

Mena smiled. "What do you mean?"

"It was a storm that came through. A pretty bad one. Chris had quite a few shingles blow off over the kitchen. I had fallen asleep on the couch. Dad woke me up around one o'clock."

"At night?"

Chase nodded. "Technically the morning ... I guess he was closing up and he looked outside and could make out Chris outside. So he wanted me to go over with him. See if Chris needed help."

Mena smiled. "Like you did in our storm."

"Pretty much. But without the tree threatening to fall through to the living room," Chase said. "But we went over. It was dark, pouring rain. Like buckets. Wind blowing. In about a half hour we had a tarp laid over that part of his roof and he invited us inside. It was early in the season so there weren't many people there yet. The summer was always my dad's least favorite time here. Now without him ... this winter is going to really be rough."

Mena leaned over to put her hand on Chase's knee. "I'm so sorry," she whispered.

He offered an appreciative smile before continuing. "That time with Chris was the most I'd ever talked to him up to that point. Him and my dad found out fast that they had so much in common. Like any subject one brought up the other had so much to contribute to the conversation. Eventually I had to excuse myself. I could barely keep my eyes open. When I woke up around ten the next morning, they were already out there getting to work. My dad was on the roof, hammering down some new shingles. Chris was on the ladder, watching. When I walked over, I swear it was like those two had known each other their whole lives. Turns out neither one had gone to sleep that night. They'd sat up the whole night talking. And from then on ... they were kind of inseparable. I loved Chris right away because I could see when he looked at my father that he got it. You know? Like he really got my dad. He got his heart. His kindness. He got what I'd always felt. That my dad really just wasn't meant for a world this ... cold. This cruel. And then one night, around the end of June, my dad asked if we could talk. So we sat down and he said that he thought Chris really liked him. I agreed, of course. It wasn't like he tried to hide it. I mean Chris didn't do anything but, like I said, it was just in his eyes when my father would be talking. Your grandfather would just hang on each word. He'd always end up smiling. Like just the sound of Dad's voice made him so happy."

"I love hearing this," Mena said sincerely. "So you told your father that you'd already picked up on Christopher's feelings?"

Chase smiled as he nodded. "Yeah. I have to admit though that I wasn't prepared for him asking me how I'd feel if he reciprocated those feelings. I'd just never thought about my dad being homosexual or bisexual. Thankfully I hadn't thought about my dad in any sexual capacity," he said with a little laugh. "But, like I said, I'd known there was something. Now ... I had all the pieces to the puzzle and it started to slowly make sense."

"What did you say to him?" Mena asked.

"I said that the only thing that mattered to me was him being happy, and if his relationship with Chris, whatever it ended up being, made him happy then ... he had my complete support."

"That must have meant so much to him."

Chase nodded. "He cried. It scared me because he cried so hard. But I guess if he'd been holding all of that in for most of his life ... I just can't imagine how that must have felt. To be able to talk about his true feelings and know that I still loved him like crazy."

"And that was the start?"

"That was it. In the beginning Dad would kind of tell me the things Chris was saying. He talked a lot about Roberta ... how much he loved her ... things like that. Chris and I didn't have too many one on one conversations. It was him and Dad. But by August, we were the three amigos. We were family. And it just grew from there."

Mena sighed, sipping her wine, the music still playing in the background. "I wish I'd known. I wish I could have been there for him. For all of you."

Chase smiled. "It would have given you some great memories to be holding on to right now."

"Did my grandfather and your father always live in their separate houses?"

"Christopher didn't really like the winters here. Plus the cottage didn't have any heat source. So he'd stay down here as long as he could. Usually staying in this house at night. Especially once the nights started to get chilly. But when Dad and I went to work, Chris always went to his cottage. And then just before the first snowfall he'd go back to Pennsylvania. Then we'd see him again in March."

"Did your father work construction with you?"

"He worked construction, but he always worked on building homes for people who were struggling. Or doing repairs for people that couldn't afford the prices of repairmen or carpenters. So ... he didn't make much money. I started working with him when I was seventeen. I'd take some bigger jobs to bring in the money we needed, and finally I was able to really start our own business. Harper Construction."

"So you ...," Mena thought back to their first conversation where he said he worked in construction. She had no idea that what he meant was that he owned his own company. That explained how she was able to monopolize so much of his time without causing him to lose his job. "Your own company. That's amazing. It speaks of a lot of hard work."

Chase nodded. "We had some lean years. But the busier I got, the happier my dad could be with his outreach in the community. Maybe someday, if you want, I can show you some of the houses he built. He meant a lot to so many people. He started having some problems with his back when he got older so he couldn't do as much. I was really glad he had Chris, because instead of feeling like he had outgrown his usefulness, he looked at the positive of having more time with the person he loved. So then it was me heading off to work and the two of them heading down to the store for their morning coffee and breakfast. Rose always took good care of them."

Mena put her wine glass down on the table beside her chair and looked over at Chase. His hair had long since dried and was back to hanging in wavy strands in front of his shoulders. "Thank you so much for talking to me about all of this."

He smiled. "It's nice to have someone that cares enough to hear it."

"So, my grandfather ... you said that his plan was to fix up the cottage. That he didn't want to sell it. But with you and your father being right here ... Didn't he want to live with Steven?"

Chase nodded. "He was starting to have trouble with the stairs to our house. We were going to make changes so that he could get in easier."

"So ... what about the cottage?"

"To be honest, I don't know. He wasn't going to sell it, I know that. But he always said that he had his plan. He probably talked about it with Dad, but he never told me the overall picture. We only talked about the actual details of making the improvements."

Mena turned her eyes to the front windows. Even though it was dark and she couldn't see beyond the rain spotted glass to the cottage that sat across the street, she could still picture it.

"What are you thinking?" Chase asked.

She took a moment before answering. "Do you ever wonder if you're doing the right thing? Like if your dad is watching and nodding. Agreeing with how you're spending your days?"

Chase let out a small laugh. "I'm pretty much doing the same things I did when he was here, so ... he's not surprised if he's watching me, that's for sure. Are you ... wondering about something? Someone?"

"I just ... I have these moments of thinking I've discovered my purpose in life and then ... it disappears under this huge weight of self doubt and disappointment."

"Disappointment in what?"

"Myself. I mean hearing you talk about your father ... he spent his life trying to make other people's lives better. You came over in the middle of the night to help somebody you didn't even know ... I just try to think sometimes. Like what am I doing that's not completely about myself?"

"Well ... you gave life to another human and raised her. I'd say that's just about the most important thing you can do in the world."

"Millions of women do that," Mena said with a smile.

"But they don't all do it well. And the children they raise do not become adults to be proud of or to be respected. So the fact that you've put an intelligent, kind person out in the world is quite an accomplishment."

"How do you know?"

"Know what?"

"That's she's intelligent and kind?" Mena asked softly.

"Well ... because ... she's your daughter," Chase answered with a shrug.

Mena watched him for a second before she smiled and stood up. "I think I need to go up to bed. If you don't mind?"

"No. Of course," Chase answered, quickly standing up as well. "Will the music bother you?"

"Not at all," Mena answered honestly. "Music helped me get to sleep for quite a few years."

They stood awkwardly for a moment, as if not sure what the proper thing to do was after sharing so much. Finally Mena just smiled and said,

"Okay, I'm going to head up. Thank you again, Chase. For everything."

"It's my pleasure. Thank you for your company," he said quietly.

"Goodnight," Mena said.

"Goodnight."

CHAPTER TEN

The next morning was spent emptying the rest of Christopher's things out of the cottage so that the initial round of renovations could begin. At lunchtime Chase made the suggestion that they walk down to the store for lunch and say their seasonal goodbyes to Rose.

"I can't believe she let me go on about my grandfather and never mentioned your dad," Mena said as they walked down the road. "She's a good friend."

Chase nodded. "We look out for each other."

"She has really nice things to say about you. Not to mention that she thinks you're very handsome."

Chase laughed. "Did she ask if you'd marry me? She's been trying to marry me off since I turned eighteen."

Mena laughed. "Kind of a mother figure for you?"

"I guess. The closest I had down here anyway. They don't come much better than Rose."

They reached the store and went inside, that same bell announcing their arrival.

"Well you two coming in here together? Anything I should know about?" Rose called out from behind the counter.

"See? What did I tell you?" Chase asked with a laugh. "Rose, Mena's married. Don't go starting rumors." He walked over to the counter and jumped over it so that he was standing in front of the owner. He put his arms around her and gave her a tight hug. "I'll miss you, Rosie," he said softly.

She returned the hug, kissing his cheek. "I'll miss you too, Chase. You can always come to Florida with us."

He smiled as he stepped back. "Who would watch over Brandford?"

Rose looked over at Mena. "We go through this song and dance every year. I never get him to come with me—"

"And I never get her to stay," Chase cut in.

Rose pointed to a vase filled with a beautiful assortment of colored roses. "You don't have to do that every year either, Chase," she said but now the laughter was gone and tears were in her eyes.

"Did you get her those flowers?" Mena asked, walking over to the counter and leaning in close to smell them. "They smell so good!"

"Every year on my last day I get a delivery of a beautiful bouquet of roses," Rose explained. "With a card that says 'Thank you. Until next year. Love, Chase'," She wiped the tears that had now fallen to her cheeks. "I don't like thinking of you being here alone." She looked at Mena. "Unless ...?"

"Oh," Mena said, looking from Rose to Chase and then back again. "I'll be here for a little while. We're just getting started with the cottage."

"Well there's that at least," Rose said before hugging Chase again. "Don't forget to call on Liz if you need anything. And the winter will go by before you know it. Of course if it gets too cold for you this year, you show up on my doorstep any time you want. Do you hear me?"

Chase smiled. "I hear you, Rose. And I promise you that I will. But if I make it through, I promise to keep an eye on the store for you."

"Like you always do," Rose said, kissing his cheek again before holding his face in her hands. "You deserve happiness, Chase. Don't you ever forget that. You are the kindest, most beautiful man I have ever had the privilege of knowing. And there is nothing that says you have to stay here this year."

"It's my home, Rose," Chase said with a little shrug. "Where else would I go?"

"Florida!" Rose said with a smile. "You call me every now and then, okay? Please? Let me know how you're doing."

"I promise you that I will," Chase said. "Now, before you start crying again, is there anything I can help you with so that you can get to your fun in the sun?"

Rose shook her head. "No, everything's done. Was just waiting for my Chase Harper visit. Now that I've gotten it, I'll close up for another year." She put her arm around his waist as they walked out from behind the counter to join Mena. "You know what I think, Mena?" she asked.

"What do you think?" Mena asked with a smile.

"I think that good ol' Christopher knew exactly what he was doing when he gave you that cottage."

"Sometimes I think the same thing," Mena said. "I don't know how but …" She could only shrug.

Rose nodded. "Yes he did." She gave Chase another hug before pulling Mena into a tight embrace. "Will I see you in the spring, Mena?"

"Yes. I'll be bringing my daughter with me. I can't wait to introduce her to you."

"And I can't wait to meet her," Rose said, her eyes filling with tears again. "Okay, you two. Go on. Get out of here. Stupid roses. I think I'm getting allergic to them."

Chase smiled, kissing the top of her head. "Safe travels, Rosie. See you in the spring. I love you."

"I love you too, Chase. Now go!"

Chase motioned for Mena to go first before following her to the door. He stopped one last time to give Rose a wave before they walked back out into the sunshine.

"Everybody loves you so much," Mena said quietly.

"Actually they loved my father and it just kind of … rubbed off on me by my sheer close proximity to him."

Mena turned to look up at Chase's handsome profile. "I don't think so. But I can tell that you don't like to be complimented so I'll let it go. For now."

"Appreciated," Chase said, looking down at her with a grin as they walked.

"Each time I walk down this road I always think about being a kid. I'd hold my father's hand, skipping beside him, singing songs." She smiled. "I have to say that he never told me to be quiet. And I think I would have even gotten on a saint's nerves. I sang constantly." Her smile slowly faded. "I have so many nice memories ... I don't know why I forget to see them when I'm talking to my parents these days."

"Maybe you'll learn to let them back in," Chase offered. "So what did you sing?" he then added with that same grin.

"What didn't I sing? If I heard it, I sang it. So pretty much the top 40 of the seventies," Mena laughed.

Chase stopped walking and turned to face Mena. "I just thought of something we could do tonight. Do you want to go out for dinner?"

"Well we did get a lot of work done already today," Mena answered with a smile.

"Right! So ... is that a yes?"

"Absolutely. Was that what you thought of? Going out to dinner?"

"Sort of. You'll have to wait and see for the rest," Chase laughed. "Come on. I'll race you!"

And with that, the man took off at an impressive run down the road, leaving Mena standing there, watching after him. As if the universe was reminding her that just maybe she watched a little too long, her phone showed that a call from Tyler was coming in. She let out a sigh and started walking before answering.

"Hello?"

"I wasn't sure you'd answer. It's been pretty quiet on your end," Tyler said. "How are you doing, Me? I've been worried about you. It's been a week."

She was quiet for a moment before answering. "I'm okay, Tyler. How are you?"

"How am I? I'm terrible, Me. I miss you. I want you to come back home. How long is this going to last? You said you'd only be gone a few days."

"Tyler, please don't," Mena said softly, her steps coming to a stop.

"Don't what? Tell you that I want you here? With me? Why can't I say that? You're my wife ..."

Mena closed her eyes, feeling her life crashing down on the peace she'd actually begun to feel. "Yes, I am your wife, Tyler. Legally. But I came here to think, remember?"

"So tell me about what you're thinking! Tell me anything, Mena!"

"Tyler, we'll talk when I get home. Okay? Please give me this time.

You owe me this."

"I owe you this? Is that how it's going to be from now on, Me?" Tyler asked. "Can't we get past it? I'm sorry. I'm so sorry. I just want to move on. Can't we do that? I want things to go back to the way they were before."

"Well ... before you were sleeping with Nikki so ... no, I can't say I have too much interest in things going back to how they were before, Tyler."

Chase appeared out from their road again. "Mena? Everything okay?" he hollered to her.

She pointed to her phone and he stood there, watching. Waiting to see if she was alright.

"Who was that?" Tyler asked. "Was that a man calling your name?"

"Yes. Yes it was. It was my friend."

"So you've been down there for a week and you've already made a friend? A guy friend?"

"I'm going to go now, Tyler. I left so that things didn't get uglier between us. After I've thought things through I'll come back and we'll talk. Okay? Just ... please give me this time. Please, Ty."

"I don't see where I really have a choice, do I?" Tyler asked.

"Goodbye, Tyler," Mena said, disconnecting the call, and putting her phone back into her pocket. She started walking again, but couldn't stop the tears. She was hiding in Brandford, and just the sound of Tyler's voice brought all of the pain right back again.

Chase apparently sensed something was wrong and started a jog back down the road to meet up with her. When he did he gave her a little smile.

"Everything okay?" he asked, turning to walk beside her.

"That was Tyler. My husband. Wanting us to just go back to normal and upset with me that I can't say that I'll do that," Mena said, the tears falling.

"I'm so sorry, Mena," Chase said, reaching out and rubbing her shoulder.

"Thank you. I don't know why I'm crying. I shouldn't have even answered the phone. This is what always happens. And I just don't know how he can't understand how the chances of me being okay enough to let our marriage continue are practically non-existent. He's not my Tyler anymore. He's this new Tyler who ... I wouldn't have married. I want him to be my

Tyler, but anything he says, or anytime I look at him ... he's not there. And some of my friends tell me that I have to forgive him, and I have. I honestly have. But forgiving doesn't mean that I can spend the rest of my life looking at him across the dining room table." She stopped, looking up at Chase. "I'm sorry. I'm rambling and ... you don't need to hear this kind of thing."

"I'll listen to whatever you need to get out," Chase answered sincerely. "How about if we do dinner another night. Maybe this is a good day for you to just ... relax in the house. Think about what we're going to do with the cottage."

"No!" Mena answered quickly. Still looking up at Chase. "Please, no. I need to go out. If I stay in the house all I'll do is think about my call with Tyler and finding out about Nikki."

"Nikki?" Chase asked but then nodded. "Oh. Nikki."

Mena nodded in response as they started to walk again. "Unless you're afraid that I'll be a wet blanket. If you do, I'll completely understand."

Chase laughed. "No. I was not worried that you'd be a wet blanket. Dinner it is then." As they turned onto their road he added, "Would you like me to invite Liz and Michael?"

"Michael? I can't believe I didn't think about Liz having another half."

"Yes. She has a Michael. Would you like to make it a group outing?"

Mena smiled as she wiped her cheeks. "You know what? That sounds perfect. It really does. Because what could be a better distraction from Nikki than dinner with three friends. Even if Michael doesn't know he's my friend yet," she added with a little laugh.

Chase laughed, taking out his phone.

"Tell her I said hello. I'm going to go in and grab a shower." And now it was Mena's turn to take a little jog away from Chase. Leaving him alone in the middle of the sandy road.

The pick up truck pulled into a dusty parking lot. When it came to a stop Mena leaned her head to the side to look at the neon sign.

"Jack Russell's. Chase, is this a bar?" she asked with a little laugh. "Did you think I needed to drown my marital woes in a few beers?"

Chase shook his head, smiling. "They actually serve really good food. And now that the season is over, it's not packed so I figured we could relax and just enjoy getting away from everything for a few hours."

He jumped a little when there was a knock on his window.

"Are you two getting out or are you going to sit in there all night?" came Liz's voice. "Let's go!"

Mena waved at her before hopping out of her side of the truck. She walked around the front and gave Liz a hug. "I'm so glad you guys could come."

They started to walk, Liz's arm staying around her shoulders. "We aren't leaving until you sincerely feel better, or are just too drunk to remember why you were sad," she laughed.

Mena looked over her shoulder to where Chase and a man that she assumed was Michae walked behind them. "You don't keep secrets very well, do you, Mr. Harper?"

"I didn't say a word except you were feeling down," Chase said. "Scout's honor."

"You weren't a scout," Liz laughed.

"Lizzie may have started drinking without you," Michael said.

Mena tried to reach a hand back. "Hi, I'm Mena."

Michael laughed, shaking her hand as best he could. "Nice to meet you, Mena. I'm Michael. I've heard a lot about you."

The foursome walked inside where a handful of others were already enjoying food and drinks. The bartender looked over and smiled, giving them a wave.

"Harper! How's it going!"

"Hi Jake. It's going alright. Okay if we grab a table for dinner?"

"Help yourselves. I'll send somebody right over."

"Thanks, man." Chase pointed to a table along one of the walls. "How about that one over there?"

With everyone in agreement, they reached the table, the men pulling out the chairs for the two women.

"What gentlemen we have," Liz said with a smile. "Thank you."

"Thank you," Mena said more quietly to Chase.

A young woman came up to the table almost immediately. "Can I start you all off with some drinks?" she asked.

"Could we just have four beers?" Liz asked, getting the response in before anyone else. "Whatever's on tap."

Mena laughed. "Make that three beers and one soda please? Coke or

Pepsi."

"Boo. Party pooper!" Liz said laughing before turning to Michael. "Should we get the karaoke started?"

"Babe, we just sat down. I told you that you shouldn't have started drinking before we got here." Michael looked over at Mena with a little smile. "She always does this on the day Rose leaves."

Mena reached over and patted Liz's hand. "We'll all miss her."

"But only until April!" Chase pointed out. "So go on up there and sing one for Rose!"

"Yeah?" Liz asked. "Mikey? Come up with me?"

"Of course."

The two got up from the table, Chase and Mena both smiling as they watched after them.

"Are they married or …?" Mena asked Chase.

"No. Poor Mike. He's been asking her for almost five years now. She still hasn't let him put that ring on her finger."

"Why not?"

Chase shrugged. "She said that when people get married, they stop being friends. She's terrified that he'll leave her."

"I guess hearing my story makes her think she's right. But … she's so wrong."

Chase looked at Mena for a moment. "Really?"

"Are you serious? Of course."

"Even with what you're going through right now, you'd still encourage somebody else to get married?"

"Absolutely," Mena answered with a nod. "What Tyler did was awful, but that doesn't mean that I'd never get married again. He's hurt our relationship, but not all relationships. Marriage is wonderful. I was very happy for a very long time. I'll be sad to not be somebody's wife. Somebody's partner."

"You sound … like your mind is really made up."

Mena's eyes widened. "Yeah, but no. … I mean I'm just saying …"

She was blessed with the opportunity to not have to answer by the beginning notes of 'You're The One That I Want' starting.

Chase laughed before hollering, "Woo!" pumping his fist in the air as Michael began to sing. His voice a bit shaky and unsure.

Mena was clapping along as Liz began singing too, the couple obviously having so much fun with each other. The other people in the bar were now all turned toward the small stage, enjoying the non-married couple doing their best John Travolta and Olivia Newton John.

"They should not be singing in the condition Liz is in," Chase said, leaning closer to Mena so that she could hear.

She laughed, nodding. "I think she's having so much fun she doesn't care."

Chase looked into her eyes and smiled. "Want to have our own fun when they're done?"

"You mean us go up there?" Mena asked, her eyes widening. "Oh no. Uh uh." Shaking her head.

"Why not? Aren't you the one that sang her way through childhood?" Chase asked, still smiling.

"Well that's different. These people weren't there," she answered, looking around the bar. When her eyes returned to Chase and saw he was still smiling, she said "Wait! Is that why you chose this place? Nice try."

Chase laughed just as the waitress returned with their drinks. The song ended and everyone applauded the valiant Grease effort, the songbirds returning to the table. Each picked up their glass of beer, taking a drink before sitting down.

"That was great!" Mena said.

"I don't think we'd make it through to the next round if we were on American Idol," Michael laughed.

"Speak for yourself," Liz said, before leaning in and kissing him softly, her arms around his neck. "I love you," she whispered.

"I love you," Michael said, pushing a strand of hair back from her face.

The waitress quietly cleared her throat. "Can I get any of you something to eat?"

"Do you like club sandwiches?" Chase asked Mena who nodded. "Can we have two club sandwiches and some fries."

"I'll have a cheeseburger and fries," Liz then announced.

"A grilled cheese and whatever your soup is today," Michael said, completing the table's orders.

Chase stood up, offering his hand to Mena. "Come on. Our turn."

Mena shook her head, looking terrified. "Chase, no. I can't go up there."

"Oh yes you can, girlfriend. Go!" Liz said, walking around to 'help' Mena up from her chair.

Mena felt like her legs were going to sleep as she walked beside Chase up onto the little stage.

"What do you want to do?" Chase asked. "I'm game to try anything."

"Well ..." Mena began looking through the available tunes. "They have some different ones on here." She broke into a smile. "Here you go. I found one for you. I was going to say we should do Donny and Marie, but no. Here it is. 'Listen To Her Heart'."

"No way. Really?" Chase asked, leaning closer to see. "That's cool. But you know, the song is really a double vocal through just about the entire thing so ..." He grinned and handed her a microphone when he picked up his own. "I hope this is a Petty crowd in here tonight."

The song started and Mena's nerves grew more out of control with each note. But somehow, when Chase started singing, she looked at him and it was as if they were the only two people there. Like they were walking together down the sandy Brandford road. His voice was beautiful and she enjoyed singing along with him. Providing, what she hoped, was an okay harmony. They sang the whole song together and she ended up having so much fun that she hated it being over.

"Let's do another one!" she hollered, making Chase burst out laughing.

"You're fun," he said. "Okay one more."

Mena returned once again to the list and looked at him with a smile. "This one. I used to sing it with my sister on the porch of the cottage."

"Mockingbird?" Chase asked as he saw where she was pointing.

Mena nodded. "Please?"

"Hey, I'll give it a try," Chase said with a shrug. "Let's go."

And they did, getting the whole bar's attention when they started.

"Mock"

"Yeah"

"Ing"

"Yeah"

"Bird"

"Yeah"

"Yeah"

"Yeah"

"Mockingbird"

Mena went from being a bundle of nerves to having more fun than she'd had in so long. When she returned to her seat, she couldn't wipe the smile from her face.

"No fair. You got to sing with the guy who can actually carry a tune," Liz said before kissing Michael again. "Just kidding, honey," she said before mouthing to Mena 'No I'm not'.

Mena laughed, but then looked at Chase. "You can sing. Like … really sing."

He smiled. "Why thank you. You're not so bad yourself."

"No, I karaoke sing. You're like … talented."

Again he smiled, but it was obvious he wanted to change the subject. He did so by turning to Michael and asking him how his latest run had been. The question caused Mena to look at Liz.

"Run? What does he do?" she asked quietly.

"He drives a truck for a living," Liz answered. "He just got back last night."

"He seems really sweet. Chase said you've been together for a while?"

Liz nodded. "He's my guy. I love him like crazy."

"But … you won't marry him?"

Now Liz shook her head. "We're good. Just like this."

"I think you should give the idea a chance. You deserve to have it all," Mena said, reaching out and squeezing Liz's hand.

"I do have it all. Besides, you're married and look at how unhappy that's making you. It's not always a fairytale."

"It is with the right person," Mena said.

Liz looked from Mena to Chase and then back again. "Well I happen to know a real Prince Charming if you ever want to give it another go," she said with a smile.

Mena turned to look at Chase as he talked and laughed with Michael.

As if feeling her eyes on him, he turned and gave her a little smile but then asked, "Everything okay?"

She nodded slowly, but couldn't be sure if that was the truth. "I was just thinking … maybe I'll have a beer after all," she stammered, hoping that her cheeks weren't blushing as badly as they felt.

"Oh okay. I'll get it for you," Chase said, quickly getting up and going to the bar.

"See?" Liz laughed. "I knew it. You think so too!"

CHAPTER ELEVEN

Mena rolled over with a groan, pulling the blanket up over her head against the bright sunlight that was winning the fight with the curtains. Different noises found their way to her. Hammers. Saws. Music. Laughter.

"Oh my gosh it's too early!" she grumbled, her face pressed against her pillow. She reached her hand out from under the blanket to get her phone off of the nightstand and quickly brought it back under. She turned her phone on and her eyes widened when she saw the time. 11:47 a.m.! She let out a little scream! When was the last time she'd slept in past nine? Or slept in at all? She was always the first one up and showered in her house. A smile on her face while Tyler and Gemma were still frowning at having to get up for school and work. Now, Mena has one night where she stays out late and her body feels like it needs several more hours of sleep in the morning to make up for it.

"Shoot. This isn't good!" she mumbled to herself as she sat up. She scrolled through several messages from Gemma and Liz. Apparently before she'd gone to sleep, Mena had felt it necessary to post online Liz's video of her karaoke duet with Chase. Why would she do that? That was the last thing Tyler should ever see. Mena knew it was innocent, but it would be hard to blame him if he was upset. She certainly would be if their places were reversed. But apparently Gemma had gotten a kick out of it. Her texts amounting to approval of their song choice, pride in Mena's ability to pull off the song, and asking why this was the first she'd seen the mysterious Chase!

"Why didn't I stick to sodas all night," Mena said to herself, hurrying into the bathroom where she hoped a quick shower would undo the haze from the night before.

When she was showered and dressed, she made her way downstairs, her apology ready to go. But she found the house to be empty. So her next choice was to follow the sound of hammering and power tools. She grabbed her sunglasses and walked out onto the deck first. Looking across the street she could see that the front door to the cottage was open. There was a truck she didn't recognize parked in front, a dumpster behind the truck, and a chair was in the small front yard with a radio sitting upon it. Apparently, with no neighbors to annoy, the volume was nothing to skimp on, as 'Life In The Fast Lane' could be heard to the water's edge. How could Chase have been right there for the same amount of time Mena had been last night, yet he was already up, out, and working?

While Mena was lost in the midst of her thoughts, a man came out of the cottage and looked up at her, giving her a little wave before walking over to the truck and getting in. Mena waved in return and then walked down the stairs and out into the street as the truck was driving away. She made her way over to the cottage, calling Chase's name over the sound of ELO's 'Do Ya' that had now replaced The Eagles.

"Chase?" she tried again as she reached the open door. "Are you in here?"

"Mena?" he called out, his voice sounding as if it were coming from the bedroom.

"Yeah. Is it safe for me to come in?"

"Sure!" he answered, now appearing from the back of the house.

"I'm so sorry for sleeping so long. That's ... so not like me," Mena began.

He responded with a smile. "No need to apologize. You obviously needed the rest. I'm glad you were comfortable. Do you want to see what we've done so far?"

Mena nodded before motioning over her shoulder. "Was that a friend of yours that I just saw leaving?"

"We work together," Chase said with a nod. "He's a great guy. Peter.

That's his name. Peter. So come here. Just watch where you walk ..."

Mena tiptoed over sawdust, drywall dust and a random nail and screw here and there. She walked to where Chase had been standing and saw that the bathroom no longer existed, nor did the wall that closed off the bedroom. The back of the house was completely open.

"Wow! And you did this in just a few hours?" she asked, unable to keep from smiling.

"Yep. It gives you an idea of how it's going to look, doesn't it?"

Mena nodded. "It looks great! I just can't believe it."

"I think the only other thing I'll do for today is take the kitchen out. Anything that you want to keep?"

"I don't think so. I think the new kitchen deserves to have new things. Don't you?"

"That's completely your decision to make."

Mena nodded again. "Yes. I definitely want new cabinets and appliances for Christopher's kitchen."

"Okay. So I'll finish that today, I'll put up the studs for the new walls tomorrow, and they'll be here on Monday to start the process of raising it."

"Just like that?" Mena asked, feeling almost giddy.

Chase nodded. "Just like that. Then once that's all done, I'll be able to work on getting everything back together inside." He did his best to sound casual as he said, "Any idea on how long you'll be here to oversee everything?"

Mena's smile faded. "You saw what just talking to Tyler did to me yesterday, so I know I'm trying to drag this out as long as possible. But I guess I'll pick out the things for the renovation. I mean cabinets, colors, lights ... things like that and then ... I'll need to go home. Handle things. But you know we'll still be in touch for ... you know, anything that comes up. It's not like I'll leave and then just expect it to be done when I get back." She tried to get the smile back on her face but was having trouble. "I didn't really think this through," she said softly.

"You're doing the best you can," Chase offered.

Mena nodded. "I guess I should get out of your way, huh? Is Peter coming back?"

"Yeah, he just wanted to go grab some lunch."

"Well ... I can be your helper while he's gone if you want. I might not look like I'm too handy, but I am. I promise. At home I was always the one doing the moving of furniture, or painting, putting things together…"

Chase couldn't help but smile. "Well okay then. How can I pass up that offer? But do you have anything other than your flip flops? Having your feet covered up might be a little safer."

"Sure thing, boss. I'll be right back!"

Mena hurried outside, singing along to the radio as she crossed the street to retrieve her sneakers. As she sat on the edge of the bed, putting them on, she took a moment to look toward the ceiling. "We're really doing it, grandfather. This is all for you." She blew a kiss and whispered, "Say hi to Stevie for me."

As she got up her phone rang and she saw Liz's name on the screen. She picked it up and answered with, "Should I whisper really softly?"

"Oh my gosh! I'm so sorry, Mena. Please believe me when I say that I'm not usually like that. I just had a bad afternoon and I … I should have known better. Forgive me?"

"Absolutely nothing to forgive, Liz. I had a great time with you and Michael, who is an absolute sweetheart by the way."

"You're so kind. Thank you. Maybe we can do it again before you go back North? Let me show you that I can have fun without embarrassing myself completely?"

"Definitely. But you weren't embarrassing. It was a lot of fun! Are you at the store tomorrow?"

"Not tomorrow. But I'll be open again on Monday.."

"Would it be alright if I stopped by? Just to say hi?"

"Are you kidding me? You stop by anytime you like."

"This time the coffee's on me."

"If you insist. And thank you, Mena. I'll see you on Monday."

"See you Monday, Liz."

Mena hung up and returned to the cottage where she was immediately given a pair of gloves and safety glasses.

"These things don't really go with the look I was going for," Mena laughed when she was all suited up for the job at hand.

"Well you look better than Pete," Chase laughed. "Are you sure you're up for this?"

"Yes. Let's do this! What first?"

"Well we might as well take this metal cabinet out first."

"Do you think that Liz could resell the cabinet and the table?"

Chase thought for a moment and then shrugged. "I don't see why not. We can put this in the back of my truck then. Let me just go back it over closer to the door."

"Okay. I'll just wait here," Mena said with a smile. Once she was alone she went around and took pictures. She had been sure to document everything since she'd first arrived and was going to make a scrapbook of it all to sit out in the cottage when it was all finished. She found herself focusing on the smallest of things. Doorknobs. Window locks. The handles on the cabinets. When she was finished, she sat down on the table and sent some to Gemma. 'Demolition Day!' she added with a heart.

'Wow, you weren't kidding,' Gemma wrote back. 'Great job! Can't wait to see it in person! Love you!!'

This time Mena turned the camera on herself and did a video of herself telling her daughter how much she loved her. Then she sent it to Gemma and laid her phone down, hearing Chase's truck outside. She hopped down and went over to the cabinet, putting all of her weight against it until it started to slide across the floor. She was almost to the front door when Chase appeared.

"Hey now. Wait a second. You're gonna hurt yourself," he said. "Sorry for taking so long. I got a call from a client that I had to take."

"You weren't gone long at all. I was just trying to be helpful," Mena said. "But I probably bit off a little more than I should be chewing. Although I did do a pretty awesome job. Right?"

"Totally awesome," Chase laughed. "But here, let me tilt it back toward me and if you could just hold up the other end that'll be good."

When Mena held the bottom of the cabinet she tried not to laugh. The entire weight of the cabinet was on Chase, yet he was pretending she was being a big help. She had to admit though, she appreciated it. It felt good to feel useful.

They walked with the cabinet to the truck that now had the tailgate down for easy access. Chase laid his end in and then grabbed the bottom from Mena and pushed it up toward the cab until it was completely inside the bed of the truck. They then did the same thing with the table before fitting the plastic chairs in around it.

"Ready to do some real demo work on those cabinets?" Chase asked with a grin.

"You have no idea!" Mena laughed.

"Wow, you really are Chris' kin, aren't you?" Chase laughed as he came out of his bedroom, seeing Mena sitting at the kitchen island, sketching intently.

She looked up at him and smiled. "I just have so many ideas for the cottage I didn't want to forget them."

He didn't take his eyes off of her as he nodded. "Just like him," he whispered. "What is it about that place?"

Mena picked up her phone. "Look. I've been looking for inspiration. I saved the pictures."

Chase took the phone from her hand and scrolled slowly through pictures of kitchens, lights, furniture, and paint colors. "You've got a good eye," he said quietly as he zoomed in on some of the pictures. "So these are your ideas for finishing the cottage?"

Mena held her pencil in her hand, nodding. "What do you think? I can see it so clearly in my mind."

"I think … it'll be beautiful," Chase answered. "Great ideas for what will be a small space. The colors you're thinking about would really open it up and play off the light to brighten it up."

Mena smiled. "Thank you. That's what I was thinking."

Chase handed her back her phone, leaning on the island. "Did you ever do this before?" he asked.

"What?"

"Design?"

Mena gave him a nod. "Yes. I actually used to have my own business, but I sold it when Gemma was small. But I still enjoy playing around with things. Not as much as I loved tearing out cabinets but it's a close second."

Chase laughed. "Yeah I think those cabinets had names and faces on them in your head. You really went to town on them. Pete couldn't believe how much we'd gotten done while he was gone." He paused. "Why did you sell your business? You're obviously very talented."

"Thank you," Mena answered sincerely. "Well … I'd had Gemma, and Tyler thought it would be better if I was home more. I tried just taking on fewer clients at first, but eventually he just felt I should sell it. Put the money in the bank for that proverbial rainy day."

"Is Chris' cottage your rainy day?" Chase asked quietly.

"I think it might be" Mena said with a slight nod. "You know, I was thinking that if I'm going to do all of this to the interior, I don't really want to reuse Christopher's furniture. Do you think it would be okay with him if I donated everything? If he were here?"

"Well if he were here, he'd probably need it so … no," Chase laughed.

"That was good. Very funny, Mr. Harper," Mena said, but she put the pencil down and looked over at her friend. "I'll need to … talk to Tyler."

Chase just watched her, nodding the slightest bit.

"If this is my rainy day," she added, with a somewhat sad smile. "Paying you, the supplies … I want him to know …"

Again Chase nodded. "What do you think he'll say?"

"I don't think he'll have a problem with it. I mean the money is from the sale of my business."

"Even if … you're leaving him? You don't think he'll fight you just to … fight?" Chase asked softly.

Mena just looked back down at her drawing, trying to keep her mind off of thoughts of what lay ahead for her.

Realizing that he wasn't going to get an answer, Chase asked, "When are you going to do that? Talk to him?"

"I … don't know. Soon, I guess," she said softly. She finally looked up again at Chase. "Could I cook dinner tonight? Would that be alright?"

"You don't have to do that."

"But if I wanted to? Would you be okay with it? It's been so long since I've cooked anything."

"I never turn down a home cooked meal," Chase answered with a smile, but it faded faster than normal. "Is it a … bon voyage dinner?".

She shook her head. "No. Not at all. I still have a few weeks, I'd think." Mena gave him a smile. "I just enjoy cooking. It relaxes me. So if it's okay with you I think I'll   just   run out to the store …"

"I need to drop our first load off at Liz's. If you want to ride along we can stop at the grocery store on the way back. It'll be quick."

"That would be nice. Thank you," Mena said. "But isn't her store closed by now?"

"I know the secret code," Chase answered with a smile. "Do you want to go now?"

"If you're ready, I'm ready."

In no more than ten minutes they were in the pick up truck, driving toward Liz's shop.

"I really hope that somebody can use my grandfather's furniture."

"Oh I'm sure that somebody is going to love being able to have them. A lot of people are struggling these days. And it feels like something Chris and my dad would have done. Like we're carrying on their traditions. Well you are. I'm just ... giving the use of my truck," Chase said with a little laugh.

"Well you're giving your truck for this trip, but what you're doing for me, in Chris' honor ... I'd say your heart has always been in service. In helping others."

"Well helping people is a lot better way to spend your time than not. Right?" Chase responded before turning the radio up a little. Wet Willie's 'Keep On Smilin' now filled the truck as Chase tapped along on the steering wheel.

"My dad loved this song," he said, humming along softly.

"I think we have the same obsession when it comes to music," Mena said with a little laugh. "I've never come across anyone who had my same eclectic taste."

"Like I said, I blame it on my father."

They both sang along to the radio as they drove the rest of the way to Liz's shop. This time, the truck pulled around to the back of the building, backing up to a garage door. Chase got out and flipped up the cover of the security keypad and quickly hit the numbers that started the garage door going up. Mena got out of the truck to help, now able to see the things that were already being stored in Liz's garage. Some of the things were in slightly better condition than Christopher's furniture, but there were quite a few pieces that looked to be a bit more worn.

Mena nodded as she looked around. "I feel good about this," she said softly, but tears came to her eyes.

Chase stood quietly for a moment before asking, "Are you sure you want to do this? We don't have to."

Again Mena nodded, tears rolling down her face. "I've been doing good, but ... it just hit me again. How I missed a whole life with my grandfather. All of these things that were his are just now ... stuff for a garage," she whispered. "Maybe I should keep it ..."

Chase walked over to her and put an arm around her shoulders as they both leaned back against the truck. "Take a deep breath," he said gently, doing it along with her. "Christopher was not a materialistic man. Things didn't mean anything to him unless he could use it to help someone else. His cottage, for all that it meant to him, what made him happy was what he could do with it. And who he could do it for."

Mena wiped her cheeks as she looked up at Chase. "Didn't he dream about it for himself?"

"Think about it realistically, Mena," Chase said, his voice still gentle and soft. "He was getting up there in years. We were going to renovate our house so that he could come and go without worrying about the stairs. But something was still on his mind for the cottage. His dream involved that cottage being with someone else in the future. This furniture ... I believe with all of my heart that what you're doing with it, is exactly what he'd want done. I don't have a doubt."

Mena nodded, her face still wet from her tears. "Thank you, Chase. I appreciate everything you said. I wish I knew what he wanted to do with the cottage once it was all fixed up. If he didn't want to sell it ... what was he going to do? Rent it out?" She shrugged slightly. "It's just ... picturing his things just being pushed in here like they were unwanted ... like he was unwanted ..." She paused. "I'm sorry for this ... emotional detour."

smiled. "It's alright. I understand. But you know ... maybe what he wanted to do with it ... maybe that's why he wrote the letter to you."

"Me? No he just wanted me to empty it out and ... take care of ... handling it. He didn't sound like he was giving it to me to live in."

"Maybe he thought he just had to get you down here, thinking you'd fall in love with it, just like he did."

Mena hung her head, trying to will the tears to stop. How could something be so emotionally overwhelming, so quickly, when it had seemed like the best idea in the world just a half hour ago.

"Do you want to do this another day?" Chase asked gently.

She shook her head. "No," she whispered. "I'm sorry. Let's do it ..."

Chase watched her for a moment and then nodded, putting the tailgate down. He climbed up into the trunk bed and handed the four chairs to Mena one at a time. After they were safely in the garage, the two took the table and cabinet off of the truck and tucked them safely into a corner of the garage as well.

"I'll send Liz a text to let her know what we dropped off," Chase said. "Are you still up for the grocery store or would you rather just grab a pizza on the way home?"

Mena quickly shook her head. "No. No, I definitely want to cook. It's exactly what I need."

"Okay then, let's go shopping," Chase said. He closed up the garage and hopped in behind the wheel of the truck. He reached his hand over to brush her's gently. "I think Chris is smiling down on you right now," he whispered.

She looked over at him and gave him a smile full of gratitude. "Thank you," she said softly.

The next leg of the drive lacked the conversation and singing of the previous leg, with Mena lost in thought. But when the truck stopped she shook herself from the tangle that was her mind.

"Oh. Wow. That was quick," she said, looking around at the somewhat empty looking parking lot. "It really gets quiet around here, doesn't it?"

Chase nodded. "It comes and goes." He turned off the truck's engine and got out, going around to help Mena. As they walked toward the store he asked, "So what are you making?"

Mena forced her mind to focus on her grocery list instead of the emotions that had overtaken her at Liz's shop. "I was going to make lasagna. If that's alright."

A smile gave Mena her answer before Chase even got out the words, "Oh that's more than alright. I love lasagna. But never make it for myself."

"I'm so glad. There aren't too many things I need so we should be able to get in and out pretty quickly."

"I would say I'm in no rush, but now that I know what's for dinner ... I'm all for hurrying," Chase laughed, grabbing a cart and following Mena inside.

As promised, the trip through the store was quick, as was the trip back to Chase's house. He put on music that played softly, and handled things pertaining to work while Mena was in the kitchen. He'd asked several times if he could help, but each time she assured him that she wanted him to just relax. When the lasagna was in the oven, Mena went to the couch and curled up.

"This is so comfortable," she said quietly. "I wish that I could just will the rest of the world away. Except for Gemma," she whispered, her arm folded on the back of the couch and her head resting against it. "I feel like I'm in a dream. And I don't want to wake up."

"You only have to wake up if you want to," Chase said, watching as she drifted off to sleep.

"You cooked that delicious meal, so I'll clean up. That's only fair,," Chase said, getting up from his chair. "Thank you so much, Mena. That has to be the best lasagna I've ever had. Hands down."

"Thank you," Mena said sincerely. "I'm glad you were here to keep it from burning. I didn't mean to take a nap. But really I've always enjoyed making lasagna. Or anything. It's just been awhile since I've felt up to it. I've had trouble getting into the mood to cook a meal. Gemma had a part time job that usually had her out of the house at dinnertime so it was kind of every person for themselves when it came to meals."

"Well, can I say that if I were Tyler, I'd be missing your cooking as much as I'd be missing you."

"You're making the assumption that he even does miss me," Mena said quietly. "Who knows?"

"Well I'd sure miss you if I was him, so, you're right. I guess I did just make that assumption."

"You're so nice. But honestly ... and I know that my emotions took a dive at Liz's ... but I really think that Tyler just doesn't like being seen as anything less than perfect. Like the world's found out that it was all a mirage. So he needs us to put everything behind us so that he can go back to being the Mr. Nice Guy that everybody loves."

Chase was scraping plates, putting the dirty dishes into the dishwasher. "Stripped bare for everyone to see. Like the Emperor and his new clothes. Can't be a good feeling."

Mena stood up, sighing as she walked over to the living room. "I guess he stripped both of us bare. Opened up our walls so that everyone could see inside. Like we're in a dollhouse now. Or a fishbowl." She stood in front of the shelves of record albums. "We need more music."

"Absolutely. Your choice," Chase said, putting the last pan in the sink to soak before starting the dishwasher, the soft hum heard in the living room when he joined Mena. "What would make you feel better? In the mood for anything in particular?"

She was running her finger along the spines of the albums. "I love how eclectic your dad's taste was. Kind of like my own. Good music is just good music. No matter how they package it to sell it to the public." She smiled. "Grand Funk. You have to be in the mood for that band. Isn't that what you said?"

Chase laughed. "No. I just didn't think that was the right background music for the talk we were having that night."

She pulled out one album and then another. "Oh this one."

"'All The Girls In The World Beware!!'," Chase said. "A fan?"

"I only had their 45's. The singles. But this album has 'Bad Time'. One of my all time favorite songs. Do you mind?"

"That it's one of your favorite songs?" he asked with that grin that Mena had come to know so well.

"That I put it on?"

Chase smiled. "Not at all. Whatever makes you happy. Do you want a drink?"

"Sure. Could I just have some more iced tea?"

"Coming right up."

Chase walked back to the kitchen as Mena carefully removed the album from its cover, the edges pressed against her palms as she placed it gently onto the turntable. She tilted her head so that she could perfectly place the needle at the start of song number four on side two. In no more than a second Mark Farner's voice filled the living room, along with Chase's who couldn't help himself from singing along.

He walked back in with a glass of tea for Mena and a bottle of beer for himself. "Good tune," he said, moving slightly to the music before sitting down in his chair.

Mena was swaying in front of the turntable, immediately able to remember so many things that were going on when she listened to this song as a young girl. "I remember being in the car while we were getting gas. Just my dad and me had gone out. He was outside the car. It was one of the first self-serve gas stations in town. And this song came on the radio. I was so in love with Mark Farner's voice."

"He's a very underrated singer," Chase said.

Mena walked over to the couch, getting her tea from Chase as she went past his chair. She sat down, tucking her legs up beside her. "We got a lot done today. I'm so sorry again for getting so upset. But I have to say that sitting here right now … it feels good to be so tired. Knowing it's from hard work." She smiled over at her roommate. "Which is probably how you feel every night."

"Tomorrow I'll take the rest of the things to Liz's if you want and then … we'll relax."

"You don't have to take Christopher's things by yourself. That's not fair."

"I honestly don't mind. Maybe it's better that you don't have to do it two days in a row. Just in case …"

"Just in case I have a meltdown again?" Mena asked with a little smile.

"Not exactly how I'd put it, but … I would rather you let me take care of it for you."

She took a moment but then nodded. "Thank you. That probably would be best." She watched him, his head now back against the chair. "Have we known each other long enough that I can ask you a question?"

He lifted his head so that he could look over at her. "Sure. Should I be worried?"

She smiled. "You asked me quite a few times during those first few days why my family never came back to this beach."

"Oh, are you finally going to tell me?"

"I want to. I don't want to keep it from you."

"Okay," Chase said, sitting up a little straighter. "But how is you telling me your story asking me a question?"

"Because … it has to do with you. Or this house, I mean."

Chase's eyes widened slightly. "You stopped coming down here because of me?"

"No. You were so young. But … something happened here one night. At your house. I woke up in the middle of the night and there were police and an ambulance. I remember my mother being worried. She made my father stay up on the porch …"

"That's not really a question," Chase said, his voice quiet. "But I think I know what the question is."

"What happened that night?" Mena asked.

"That was probably … the night my grandfather died," Chase said slowly.

"Were the police here a lot?" Mena asked with a little smile.

"No. No. I'm sure that was the night my grandfather died. He was drunk and fell. He hit his head on the table that we had in the kitchen before we put the island in. One of those things where he hit it just right. Or ... wrong, I guess is the real way you'd define that. It was just me and my dad there so we called for the ambulance and the police showed up too."

"For an accidental fall?"

"I think they have to show up for anything like that. Make sure ..."

"That you or your dad didn't kill him?" Mena asked.

"I guess. See exactly where he fell. What he'd been drinking. Stuff like that."

"Oh Chase. I'm so sorry."

"No, I'm sorry."

"For what?"

"Well, that your parents thought it wasn't safe to come back down. Instead of it just being a drunk old man who hit his head."

Mena nodded. "Yeah they ... sure had that wrong, didn't they? I wonder why they jumped right to thinking it was something dangerous or scary? I mean your grandfather was older. Why didn't they start with a heart attack or something like that?"

Chase shrugged. "Who knows. That was probably a pretty jarring sight to wake up to. I can see it shaking them a little bit." He gave Mena a little smile. "If they hadn't stopped coming down, I bet we would have become friends."

Mena returned the smile. "I bet we would have. Once I got over my crippling shy phase."

"Right. After that."

CHAPTER TWELVE

The next morning held a chill in the air that kept Mena in bed longer than normal. As usual, when she finally made her way downstairs she found that Chase had been up for hours. She was sitting at the island in her bathrobe when he walked in from outside.

"Do you ever sleep?" Mena asked with a sleepy smile.

"Some," he said, returning the smile as he walked toward the coffee maker. "You look like you could use a cup."

"Oh yes, please," Mena answered. "Would you like me to make something for breakfast after I wake up a little more?"

"Thank you, but I already ate. I had to meet somebody at a job at six so I got an early start. Help yourself to anything that's here though. Or I can bring you back something."

"Bring it back? Are you taking Christopher's things already? I can get ready and help if you give me a second. Or if you're going somewhere else ... ?" Mena asked, but then quickly realized she was probably overstepping. "I'm so sorry. It's none of my business."

Chase laughed. "Hey, I'm an open book. I have to check out another one of my jobs and then, I have the rest of Chris' things already loaded into the truck, so I was going to drop everything off afterwards."

"I can go with you for Chris' things. I can help. Really. I'm sorry for yesterday …"

"It's alright. I got it. You just relax. Remember, today is your day off."

"What about you? You have to work today? Who would expect you to be on the job on a Sunday?"

"Oh I don't mind. Remember, I'm usually here by myself, so being busy isn't a bad thing."

"Oh. Right. Sorry. Again," Mena said as he handed her a mug filled with hot coffee. "Well if you don't like days off then I don't either. Are you sure you don't want me to come with you?"

"I'd love your company, but I won't be long. What can I bring back? I'll be passing just about everything."

Mena thought for a moment, realizing that she was kind of hungry. "Some pancakes? From anywhere. If you hit a McDonald's drive thru?"

"You got it. So you'll be okay?"

"Absolutely. I might even still be in my bathrobe," Mena laughed.

Chase laughed as well as he took one last sip from his own coffee cup. "You have my number. Call if you have any trouble."

"You do the same," Mena responded with a smile.

He stood by the island for a second as if he might say something, but instead he finally headed for the door and left Mena alone in his house.

She went over to the turntable and started the record playing that had been on before she'd gone to bed the night before. Boz Scaggs' 'Lowdown' filled the room as she curled up on the couch with her coffee, looking out the window at Christopher's cottage. Soon she was lost in thought …

… "Okay who's ready to go swimming?" Patton Weatherly asked as he emerged from the cottage's bathroom in swim trunks and a tshirt. "Pris? Shawn? You want to walk down to the water with me? Willie?"

As usual Mena had been listening to her radio.

"Kids, come on. Go with your father," Diana said, waving her arms as if she could physically 'shoo' everyone from the room.

"Can't I stay here?" Mena asked. "I'm listening to The Guess Who."

"I give up," Diana says. "But it doesn't matter who it is. Go down to the beach with your father."

Mena looked over at her father who gave her a little grin. She sighed before getting up and going over to him, taking his hand.

"Your mother never really was up on the good bands," he said softly, giving her hand a squeeze. "Who's on now?"

"'Lucy In The Sky With Diamonds'," Mena answered, the earphone keeping anyone else from hearing her music.

"The Beatles?"

"Elton John."

"A solid cover," Patton assured her as she slipped into her flip flops, grabbed her towel and walked by his side to the sand.

When they crested the little hill at the end of the road, she hurried down on the sand, picking out the perfect spot to sit and watch her father swimming. She spread out her towel and sat down on it, having no interest in getting in the water herself.

"Keep an eye on these for me," her father said as he took off his tshirt and sneakers, leaving them by Mena's towel.

"Okay, Dad," Mena assured him.

Priscilla spread out a towel next to Mena's and laid down on it in her bikini. "You can take out your earphone."

"Okay," Mena said, unplugging the earphone from the jack and putting her radio down on her towel between them.

"I'm going to marry a rock star one day," Priscilla said, her eyes closed.

"Like Elton John?" Mena asked.

"Like Robert Plant."

Mena nodded. "Neat."

Shawn came running from behind them toward the water, another boy at his side.

"Hey Priscilla," the boy said.

Priscilla opened her eyes, shading them with one hand. "Oh. Hey Chase," she said before closing her eyes again.

"Don't be gross, Chase," Shawn said, grabbing the boy by the arm as they continued running to the water. "Hey Dad, we have a football!" he hollered.

"That boy likes you," Mena said to her sister as she watched the boys having a catch in the water with her father.

"He's just a kid," Priscilla said. "And he's no Robert Plant." …

... Mena sat up a little straighter, not sure where that memory had come from. How she had always loved talking music with her father. When they stopped, she couldn't pinpoint. But she suddenly missed it.

And Chase.

She smiled. She wished she'd had more memories of him. But back then she'd been more interested in her radio then she was in 'strangers'. And he was more interested in Priscilla. But Mena was sure he was right. They would have been friends. The best of friends.

When her coffee was finished she turned off the record and switched on the radio instead. Choosing the oldie's radio station that she'd come to love during her time in Brandford. Once music was again filling the house she went upstairs to shower. When she was finished she cleaned and straightened up the house. With the exception of Chase's room. That door had remained closed and she would never dream of invading his privacy in that way. She was putting dishes away, dancing to Ringo Starr's 'It Don't Come Easy' when she heard the door close. She jumped and spun around in almost one motion. When she saw Chase with his phone up to his ear she hurried to the stereo and turned down the volume.

"Sorry," she mouthed to him.

He shook his head slightly, motioning to her that it was fine as he spoke, "I was at the Victor job just now. The cabinets came in so we can head over there tomorrow." He listened for a moment, putting the bag he'd been holding on the counter before saying, "Reg can get the crew started on Kincaid. I want to get the cabinets put in for Victor." He nodded. "Great. I'll see you in the morning, Pete." He put his phone down on the kitchen island and smiled at Mena. "A Ringo Starr fan?"

"Oh you know me. I can't stand still when I'm listening to the classics," Mena laughed. "I couldn't help but overhear, sorry. Sounds like you're pretty busy. You know that there's no rush on the cottage, right? I mean ... you have an actual business to run and ... Victor, I've heard you say that name a lot since I got here ... Rose mentioned them too ..."

"Yeah, that's a project that's just taking too long. I can't pull the guys off of our other jobs so I just try to grab some time whenever I can."

Mena knew how stupid her question was going to sound, but she asked it anyway. "Is there anything I can do to help? It's probably my fault that you don't have as much free time as you did before I got here."

Chase gave her an appreciative smile. "Do you know how to hang cabinets?"

"Not yet, but I'm happy to learn," Mena answered honestly. "If it would help."

"That's really nice of you. It is. But no. As of today I don't need to put you to work. Now if it was demo ..," he laughed.

"Oh yeah, I've got demo down. Just give me a sledgehammer and point me in the right direction. I'll destroy anything you want me too." The words that she was going to say next were cut off when the next song on the radio started. Eric Clapton's 'Layla'. "Oh … Oh I love this song." She turned the volume up again, letting the sound of that guitar overtake the room. She couldn't stop herself from dancing around like a flower child at Woodstock.

Chase leaned back against the island watching her, starting to sing along with the chorus.

Mena held out her arms toward him as she moved and turned them through the air. He stepped toward her, playing air guitar and smiling as he continued to sing. But he stopped when he saw his phone ringing again.

"Sorry, I have to get this. I'll take it in the bedroom …," he said, grabbing his phone and heading to his room, closing the door behind him.

Mena continued to sway to the music, looking at the closed door. She couldn't remember the last time that Tyler and her had even listened to music together, much less danced to it. Something that had always been so important to her had been left by the wayside, except when she was alone in the car.

When the song ended, she turned the volume down again before walking over to the bag that Chase had brought home with him. She peeked inside to see two containers. She assumed it was the promised breakfast so she reached inside and pulled one container out, already able to smell the pancakes that she knew were hiding inside. She took the other container out as well as the plastic forks and knives, butter and syrup. She watched the bedroom door, knowing it would be rude to eat without the person that had brought the food home. Luckily she didn't have to wait long.

"Oh good you got your pancakes. Sorry. More work problems," he said, sitting his phone down again.

"I'm sorry," Mena said softly. "Do you want to talk about it? I might not know construction, but I'm still a good listener."

"I appreciate that, but let's just eat. And … talk about your dancing," he said with a grin.

"You liked my dancing. I know you did," Mena said seriously, starting to dance again, this time to Cher's 'Dark Lady'. Then she started laughing. "I dance like I'm drugged. Like I've never danced before."

Chase laughed. "Your dancing is ... unique. But I like it. You feel the music. You enjoy it."

"Exactly," Mena said, getting plates out of the cabinet. As she put one in front of Chase she said, "I was thinking about how long it's been since I just ... had fun. Like listened to music and didn't get depressed or cry or ... I don't even know. To just enjoy music ... I've missed it so much."

"It looks good on you," Chase said quietly.

Mena looked down at her tshirt. "What?" she asked, not sure what he was referring to.

"Happiness. You look happy."

She smiled. "And I feel happy. Thanks to you."

"Me?"

"You're rubbing off on me, Harper. I've never seen you without a smile on your face. How do you do it day after day?"

"Nobody's happy all of the time," Chase answered as he started to butter the pancakes that were now stacked on his plate.

"Well you do a pretty good imitation of happy."

He gave her a little smile. "Well ... maybe I have been happy lately."

Mena stopped for a moment. "Yeah? Only lately?"

"Can we not do this?" Chase asked. "Please?"

"Mr. Harper, is there something you're not telling me?"

Chase looked up, an expression of concern on his face. "Like what?"

"Oh I don't know. I just wondered if maybe ... you ... had somebody new in your life? Somebody that was keeping a smile on your face? And if so ... they must hate me because I'm taking up all of your time."

He seemed to freeze, the knife in the air with butter slipping from the tip. "What are you talking about? Who would be in my life except ... you?"

Mena watched his face. "I'm sorry. I was just kidding ..."

"Do you really think that? That I'm seeing someone? While I move you into my house?"

"Chase, I didn't mean anything by it. You could be interested in someone. There's nothing wrong with that. I mean ... we're just ... friends," Mena said.

Chase nodded slowly. "Right. Friends. Well ... even so, there's no one in my life currently."

Mena tried to lighten the mood by reaching over and poking his cheek. "So it's just me that's making you so happy."

His eyes met hers and held them for several seconds. "You don't want me to answer that," he whispered.

Mena couldn't look away. She continued to watch him even when his eyes looked down at his pancakes. "I'm sorry," she said softly.

"For what?" he asked without meeting her eyes again.

"This. Whatever I did. Putting my foot in my mouth. I'm ... sorry. I was just ... kidding around. Trying to make you laugh."

"It's okay," Chase answered before putting a forkful of pancakes into his mouth.

"I ... don't think it is. I feel like I ruined something and ... I'm so sorry," Mena said sadly. She took her plate around the island and sat down beside him wishing she could put that smile back on his face. Apparently she was wrong and he wasn't happy all of the time. This time because of her big mouth.

They sat quietly for a moment before the radio made them both look up.

Mock ... Yeah ... Ing ... Yeah

Mena pushed her elbow against his arm. "It's our song," she said, smiling at him.

It took him a few seconds, but then his face broke into that smile that she'd come to rely on. "We did it better."

"Yes, we did, Harper. Yes we did."

But that ended up being as much as Mena got from Chase. The rest of breakfast passed rather quietly, with the exception of the music. As if trying to match the mood in the house, the muted sunlight that had tried its best to brighten the beach was losing the fight to the passing clouds that seemed to be getting the upper hand.

Even with breakfast long over and everything cleaned up, conversation continued to be at a minimum. Not to say that if Mena had said anything Chase wouldn't respond. It just wasn't like it had been before and

Mena couldn't figure out why. She watched out the front window as Chase walked over to the cottage. He wanted to make sure that everything was ready for Monday when the crew was coming to raise the house. Given his reaction at breakfast she realized how little she knew about him. She trusted him immediately upon meeting him, but most of the details of his life were still a mystery, while Mena seemed to go on and on about her own life constantly.

Maybe she talked too much.

This morning when she approached the subject of Chase being in a relationship his whole mood turned. She had hit a nerve. Yet, he had never even mentioned anyone being in his life. Rose and Liz had both said he spent a lot of time alone. Somebody as amazing as Chase deserved to have it all. He deserved to have a special relationship in his life. Maybe in addition to seeing Christopher's dreams for the cottage become a reality, her job here was also to discover whatever wounds hadn't healed enough for Chase to let someone in. To invite someone to share his life.

She grabbed a sweater and slipped it on before walking across the street herself. She found Chase around the back of the house, making sure everything had been property disconnected.

"Hey," she said as she approached him.

"Hey." He only glanced at her over his shoulder before focusing once again on the water pipe that had been capped off.

"Are we okay?" Mena asked gently. "You've been such an amazing friend to me and I'm really feeling just like ... I'm not proud of myself, Chase. I feel like I've just dumped on you, accepted all of this help and ... I'm not normally this selfish or self absorbed. I want to fix whatever I did this morning. Can I?"

He straightened up, wiping his hands on his pants before turning to face her. "Fix what? What did you break?"

Mena shrugged. Her eyes glistening with unshed tears.

"Hey," he said, walking toward her. "You're going to cry? I'm sorry."

"What are you sorry for?" Mena asked, sniffling.

"Whatever did ... this," he said quietly, reaching up to touch her face gently and wiping a tear that had fallen free. "The last thing I'd ever want to do is be the cause of tears in your eyes," he whispered.

"So I'm sorry and you're sorry ... Does that mean that we're okay?"

Chase gave her one of his beautiful smiles as he nodded. "We're okay –" His words came to an abrupt stop as he pulled his phone out of his pocket. "Sorry ...," he said as he read the text that had come through. "I'm going to have to run out and check on the Victor job again. I hate leaving after this ... meaningful conversation, but I won't be long," he said with a grin.

"Okay. Go do what you must. I'll just be here feeling selfish and self absorbed. And sorry," Mena laughed but then her tone became more serious. "Is everything alright? With work?"

Chase nodded as they started to walk back around the cottage to his truck. "Yes. The Victor project. One of the ones I had to check on this morning. The owners stopped over and have some questions."

"Your clients can get pretty demanding, huh?" Mena asked with a smile.

Chase shook his head. "No, not these guys. Couldn't be nicer. Which is why I'd hurry out on a Sunday afternoon to talk to them." He got to the truck but then patted his pockets. "I left the keys in the house," he said, going around the truck and hurrying up the stairs to the front door.

Mena did her best to keep up and while they were both standing in the kitchen she asked, "Would you like some company? If not, it's perfectly fine. It's just ... I've cleaned everything I can clean. I don't have a book to read or a mystery to solve anymore so ..."

He grabbed his full keyring off of the island, turning to look at her. "Yeah? You want to ride along?"

"Only if you want me to. Or ... you know, if it's not a problem."

"No, it's fine."

"Okay. Great. I'll shut everything off and lock up. I'll hurry and be right down."

Chase nodded before heading out the door and down to his truck.

Mena went around turning off lights. Once she was confident she hadn't forgotten anything, she locked the front door and went down to the waiting truck, climbing in the passenger side door.

"Ready?" Chase asked.

"Ready," Mena answered, locking the door and pulling on her seat belt. "And thank you for letting me tag along."

"No problem. And I really am sorry about this morning. Upsetting you."

"Ditto," Mena said with a smile. "So which direction are we heading in? Out to the highway?"

"No," Chase answered. "Actually we'll be heading this way," as he put on his right turn signal at the end of their little road.

"Oh wow, I've never been down this way. I don't think I've ever been further than our street."

"Really?"

Mena nodded. "I don't know why I always assumed it just came to a dead end."

"You tourists," Chase laughed as they ventured into Mena's admitted unknown.

"You can feel the air getting cooler," she said as they drove down the rather narrow road that had the sand creeping up on each side to the blacktop. "It's funny how fast the change comes in."

"You mean it's cooler down here than it was at the house?" Chase asked with a chuckle.

"I think you like your own jokes too much," Mena said, doing her best to not laugh.

As they'd seemed to bond over music, the radio was always playing when they were together in the truck. And this trip was no different. Elton John joined them on their journey with 'Somebody Saved My Life Tonight'.

"Another song that I belted out when I was young with no idea what a lot of the actual words were," Mena laughed, her head leaning back against the headrest. "Never stopped me though. I was confident."

"Fake it til you make it?" Chase said, glancing over at her as much as his driving would allow.

"Or just ... fake it."

Mena's head was turned to the right as she watched all of the unfamiliar homes and buildings as they drove past them. "Isn't it funny how this place always just stood still in my memories. That little few blocks of Brandford Beach. But all of this existed. Or didn't back then, but does now." Her eyes watered again. "I wish my memories were actual places I could go back to," she whispered. "I wish that I could look at the sunlight the same way. I wish I could capture that golden orange hour just before sunset and paint it over every memory. I wish that I could hear this song and turn to see my sister sitting beside me ..."

Chase continued to glance over toward her. "Are you sure you're okay?" he asked gently.

Mena nodded. "Yes. Sorry. I got emotional this morning and now the floodgates are open, I guess. I just ... miss so much. But it's all gone. And nothing is ever quite how you remember it, is it?"

"I think our memories do us the favor of making things look a little better than they really were."

Again Mena nodded. "I think you're right."

Chase put on his turn signal and made his way down a sandy driveway until they reached a home that was clearly under construction. An SUV was already there and a man got out when he saw Chase approaching.

Chase put the truck in park and turned off the engine before opening his door. "Do you want to get out or stay in the truck?"

"Is it okay if I get out?" Mena asked.

"It's fine," Chase said, climbing out and walking toward the man, hand extended. "How are you Alex?" he asked as they shook hands.

When Mena caught up she heard the other man apologizing. Apparently it was the day for it.

"I didn't mean for you to run right over, Mr. Harper."

"Chase."

The man smiled shyly. "Sorry. Chase."

"And please don't apologize. I told you to let me know right away if you didn't like something."

"No. Oh no. It's not that we don't like something. I just think that they sent you the wrong cabinets."

Mena turned when she heard another car door close. She saw a pregnant woman get out of the passenger side of the SUV.

"Well I'll definitely send them back if they're the wrong ones," Chase said, giving the woman a smile. "Hi Christine." It was as if he only then realized he hadn't introduced Mena. So he quickly said, "Alex. Christine. This is my friend Mena Prescott. I'm helping her with a project too. I hope that it's alright that she came with me too."

"I can go back to the truck ..."

But Mena quickly received smiles from Alex and Christine. They were now standing side by side, holding hands.

"He's an amazing craftsman," Alex said to Mena with such an incredible amount of sincerity.

Mena smiled. "He is, isn't he?"

"Okay, let's go in and check those cabinets," Chase said, patting Alex's arm.

"Oh Chase, I saw the bathroom floor. It's beautiful," Christine said as they walked up onto the porch.

Chase smiled. "I'm glad you like it. I thought it came out really good. Think the kids will like it?"

"Oh my goodness, yes. I can't wait until they can see it."

"I would think we can have them through by the end of the week," Chase said. "I just want to make sure that it's safe."

Christine nodded, but was clearly emotional.

Mena rubbed her arm. "Are you alright?" she whispered as they men walked inside.

"Yes. Thank you," Christine answered as they remained on the porch. "Chase is just a godsend to us and … my husband is such a proud man. But Chase is always so kind and never makes Alexander feel as if he couldn't hold his head up high. He's not used to accepting help. Especially of this magnitude."

The woman spoke with a soft accent and an unmistakable love for the man that Mena now knew to be her husband.

"There's nothing wrong with reaching out to Chase for help. It's what he does," Mena said, wanting to do anything to take that look of sadness out of Christine's eyes.

"Help?" Christine asked. "This isn't help. This is … everything. He built this house for us. He didn't tell you?"

Mena shook her head, but was beginning to understand why Rose had included this family in her list of people that Chase was helping. He obviously meant a lot to them. "I mean I know that he builds houses …"

"Our home was here once. On this land. It wasn't this beautiful, but it was ours. Alex had worked hard for many years to buy it for us. But in the early Spring, we'd had a little heater plugged in because our main heater needed to be fixed and we didn't have the money to take care of it just yet. But the baby's room was cold. I don't know if you remember, but in March we had those two weeks where the temperatures were around freezing."

"I do. Yes," Mena said softly.

"Well … something happened and the heater caught fire …"

Mena's eyes widened. "Christine, I'm so, so sorry … Your baby …"

"We all got out of the house safely but … by the time the fire trucks got here there was hardly anything left. Alex blames himself for everything. For not having a better insurance policy on the house. For the heater not working. We were in such a mess and had no home anymore … Rose at the store …"

Mena nodded.

"She heard about what we were going through. We were living here on this land in our car. Alex, me and our four kids. She would give us meals and then she reached out to families that might not be using their homes for any part of the season. She got permission for us to stay in a cottage. The owners had gone to Europe and wouldn't be back until August … She was an angel. And then next thing we know, Chase shows up at the door and says he wants to build us a house."

Mena smiled. "What a pair those two are."

"No. I don't think you understand. He's not accepting anything for all of this work. Not one cent."

Mena looked at the open door, hearing Chase speaking with Alex. "That's … wow," she said softly. "He's …"

"An angel," Christine whispered.

"Honey, come here!" Alex then called out to his wife.

"You'll excuse me?"

Mena nodded. 'Yes. Of course." She let the woman walk in first, but followed behind several steps.

"These cabinets weren't a mistake," Alex said, causing Christine to start to cry.

"Chase, we can't let you do this," the woman sobbed.

"The other cabinets weren't available any longer," Chase said, giving the woman a smile filled with so much kindness. "I remembered you liked these so I went ahead and placed the order. I'm sorry I didn't talk to you first, but I know you'd like to be in before Christmas so I wanted to get the order in as quickly as possible."

Christine looked at Chase for a moment before throwing her arms around him and hugging him tight, still crying as her head rested against his shoulder. "Thank you so much!"

Chase rubbed her back softly before she took a step back. "While we're here," he said. "Is there anything else that you've thought about that you might need in your house? Now's the time. Pretty soon it will be too late for any changes."

Both Alex and Christine stood there and shook their heads, surrounded by what would soon be their very own beautiful kitchen.

"What more could we ever want?" Alex whispered emotionally.

"Okay, boss," Chase said with a smile. "We'll be out here this week and should have the kitchen fully put together. I'll let you know as soon as there's something for you to come back and see."

Christine hugged him again while Alex shook his hand.

"Thank you, Mr. Har — Chase," Alex said.

"You are very welcome," Chase answered sincerely. "I'm going to double check a few measurements before I leave. If you need me to move my truck, just holler and I'll come right out."

"We should be fine," Alex said, shaking Chase's hand one last time.

"My angel," Christine whispered, kissing Chase's cheek before walking out after her husband.

Mena watched them walk away before looking back at Chase. "So ... you built this all yourself?" The rooms weren't terribly large but they all had the studs up as well as the drywall. It was easy for her to picture what it would look like when he turned the keys over to that lovely couple and their children. Chase had opened her up to that ability. To see the possibilities in something that others might just pass by.

"Not everything. I've had help," Chase said. "Can you hold this?" he then asked, handing her the end of his tape measure. When she took it he added, "Just hold it right there ..." He pulled the tape out the length of one wall, taking a second to quickly write down the number. "Okay, thank you."

Mena let go, watching his face. He was now looking at his phone. "I've never seen anything that you've built. You're really good. Not that I ever doubted that you would be, it's just ... to see how you create a place for someone to live, out of nothing ..."

"It's nothing," Chase said with a little smile. "Most builders would have a whole neighborhood built in the time it's taken me to try and give Alex and Christine their home."

"Well this is what you call a custom build, right? Nobody will have a home exactly like theirs. This one is built specifically for them. I think that's worth the extra time. And it seems to mean so much to them ..." She stood at the window already placed in the back wall. "Look at how pretty that view is. This is where they'll stand doing their dishes or ... whatever.

Watching kids play out there ... And it will all be because of you."

"What I do isn't exactly brain surgery," Chase said with a little laugh. "But I'm glad you like it. I just had to double check my measurement for the counter, but I'm done. So ... are you ready to go?"

Mena nodded slightly. She turned and walked through the other unfinished rooms to the front door. She went out onto the porch while Chase locked up, and then they returned to the truck.

"You really followed in your father's footsteps," she said softly.

"How's that?" Chase asked.

"You talked about how he helped people in the community. Christine told me what you're doing for her family. She calls you her angel. And I get the feeling this isn't an isolated incident."

Chase smiled, opening her door for her. "She's a sweet woman."

"Well ... I can't let you keep working on the cottage," Mena said gently before she climbed up into the truck.

"Wait, what?" Chase stammered. "Okay, what just happened?"

"You're trying to give this family a home. They lost absolutely everything. That should take precedence over a cottage that has no real timeline. It can be done anytime. I've been acting like everything is so important, but what I just saw ... that's important."

"I have time to work on Chris' cottage. He was important to me."

"Selfish and self absorbed. That's me," Mena said, pulling the door closed.

Chase walked around the truck and got in behind the wheel. "I thought we'd covered that you're neither of those things," he said, backing them out onto the road and heading once again toward Rose's store and the turn that would take them to the highway.

"Do we have to go right back?" Mena asked.

"I guess not. Is there someplace you wanted to go?"

"Usually when we came to Brandford, my family, we didn't go anywhere else. Which makes sense because it was my father's vacation. I mean the man was going all the time when we were home. So now I can understand that when we got down here he just wanted to relax. Listen to his ball games or get in the water. Spend time with his kids ..."

Chase nodded but he was clearly not sure how this conversation fit with the one that had never quite been finished since leaving the Victor house.

"But this one time, we went out for dinner. I don't even know where it was. I just remember that the building was shaped like this." She put her hands together to form a triangle. "It was dark wood. I remember that there was a door to go in but there was also a walk-up window. That's what we did. I walked up with my Dad. Mom, Pris and Shawn went to one of the picnic tables they had set up under trees. It must have cost so much money to take a family of five out for dinner, but ... we loved it. It was so much fun. Just hamburgers and hotdogs. Chips. Sodas ..."

Chase thought for a moment and then nodded again. "I think I know what you're talking about. If I'm right it was called Frank's Dog House. It closed down awhile ago but if you're up for a ride, I can take you there. See if it's the place you're talking about." He glanced over at her. "But you look a little pale, so we can do it another day too if you're not feeling good ..."

"I'd like to go now. If you don't mind. I'm feeling okay."

"No, I don't mind. But we might have to stop for some hot dogs after because now I'm hungry," Chase laughed.

"What you're doing for those people is ... amazing." Maybe it seemed like Mena had moved on to a different topic of conversation, but she hadn't. It was all still there.

He smiled while shaking off the compliment. "I'm a builder. I'm building. It's what I do."

"And what you do is amazing," Mena said. "I've had so much fun just trying to envision what Christopher's cottage is going to look like ... I can't imagine doing that with an entire house. Like just ... looking at an empty lot and then creating this beautiful home. In your mind first and then having it come to life. Especially for people like Alex and Christine. I mean what's more important to someone than having a home for their family? You give that to people. You're giving it to them."

"Right now, I'd rather build hot dogs," Chase said, his eyes sparkling with amusement as they drove down that now familiar road. Short of the highway he put on his left turn signal.

"Don't we go onto the highway?" Mena asked.

"No. That highway wouldn't have been here back then. This was the main road for decades. It's cut up a lot now, but it does go at least as far as Frank's."

"Right! On the way down I was wondering what happened to the road we used to take," Mena admitted.

They drove on in a comfortable silence, just the radio playing softly. Mena watched out the window at the sand along the roadside. The tall grass growing where homes or business once sat. The sad casualties of the building of the highway. Making it easier for more people to get to the beaches more quickly, but sadly cutting off that traffic from the smaller businesses that relied on them to survive.

"I have that feeling again," Mena said softly. She wasn't sure exactly what was happening or why her brain seemed to be tossing random thoughts around like ragdolls.

"What feeling is that?" Chase asked as he glanced over at her. "Are you okay?" he then added. "Now even your lips look kind of pale. Is that a thing?"

"I'm fine," she answered. "It's just that feeling that the past is so close I should be able to close my eyes and when I open them again it will all look like it did forty years ago. I think I've been living there too much lately. A side effect of coming back down here."

"Sometimes it probably feels safer to live in the past than to face the future," Chase said before his tone brightened up. "Look. Here. Is that what you remember?"

The truck pulled into what had once been a bustling parking lot. Now it was a mixture of stone, sand and overgrown weeds. A wooden building with a high pointed roof that extended like legs down on either side sat sadly at the far end of the lot. It had once been painted brown and now that paint was chipped off over what looked like at least more than fifty percent of the exterior. A few broken picnic tables could just barely be seen under growth that was almost as tall as Mena herself.

She opened the truck door and got out, standing in the lot, looking at the dilapidated structure. She held onto the truck for a moment before feeling confident enough that her legs would hold her up. She walked slowly toward the building, heading to what had been the walk up serving window. The slightly overcast day dissolved into a long passed warm summer night. Everything cast in that golden hue. Her father was standing ahead of her ordering dinner for his family. He was young, trim and so handsome. It dawned on Mena that he had been younger at that moment than she was today. The memory was so vivid that she could even hear 'Please Come to Boston' playing out of the speakers that were mounted in the eaves.

Mena turned her head and could see so clearly her mother, brother and sister getting settled at one of the picnic tables. Her mother was so beautiful and had a smile that was home to Mena as a child. And now she saw that smile. She almost felt as if she was back there and could get her mother's attention with a wave.

"Mena?"

Chase's voice broke the spell and Mena was once again staring at the outside of the rundown building, an autumn chill in the air around her. She felt dizzy, putting her arm out to steady herself against the chipping paint, but catching a piece of broken glass instead that went into her palm. She let out a cry.

"Are you okay?" Chase asked, hurrying over to her. "Let me see your hand."

She nodded, "I'm okay. It's just a scratch," even though it was far from the truth. Her hand was throbbing as she pulled out the jagged glass from her hand. "How do things go so far off course, Chase?" she whispered.

He put an arm around her. "You need to let me see your hand. You've turned a pretty scary shade of white."

Mena nodded. She could feel her heartbeat pounding in her hand. "I think I just need to sit down. Can we go back in the truck?"

He nodded his head, keeping his arm around her and walking with her, opening up the door for her and helping her onto the seat. It was the first glimpse he'd gotten at the amount of blood that was seeping out of her clenched hands. He walked around and got in on the other side, turning in his seat toward her. "I think we need to get you to a hospital. That's ... a lot of blood."

"I don't know that I've ever had a more vivid memory than the one that just washed over me. Like the Brandford waves," Mena said softly.

"Yeah. Okay. We're going," Chase said, tuning out the words Mena was saying, instead focusing on getting her to a doctor. The blood was now dripping onto her thighs, soaking through her jeans.

"I ... don't think I'm a good person," Mena said. "Not like you. Was I mean to my family, do you think?" She gave him a little smile. "I'm feeling a little lightheaded."

Chase reached over to put his hand on her shoulder. "It's probably from the loss of blood. But if you truly have any regrets about how things are with your family ... thankfully they are all still here. On this earth. So that means you still have time to reach out. Reconnect."

Mena immediately became defensive as the swimming feeling in her head worsened. "It's not that I think I'm a horrible person —"

Chase gave her a smile as he drove. "Of course you're not a horrible person. No fault. No blame. You just might want to ... do your part in maybe repairing those relationships, right? Maybe if you talked to them ... I mean really talked ... you'd learn things that you'd never imagine were going on in their lives. Look at what was going on in Chris's life and no one knew. His secret was love but maybe other people are hiding pain or regret ... Either way, reaching out ... maybe you'd get some answers once and for all. And just maybe you'd have a better Thanksgiving or Christmas visit this year?"

Mena looked down at her hand and her eyes widened. "That's really bleeding."

"Just don't look at it. We're almost there. Just ... keep talking," Chase suggested.

"I talked to Christine about their situation. About how you helped without letting them do a thing in return. How Rose gave them free meals ... I want to be that kind of person. But under my self imposed microscope ... I've come up so short, Chase," she whispered.

"Not from where I'm sitting," Chase answered softly.

"What if ... Tyler isn't the bad guy?"

"Mena—"

"No. No. I mean yes, he did cheat on me. But what if I just wasn't a good wife to him?"

"If you were or you weren't, it doesn't give him that right."

Mena looked over at his profile. "Have you ever said one unkind thing to anyone that wasn't in defense of someone else? Have you ever talked shit about someone behind their back? Did you ever inflate a cost sheet for a customer or not go back and pay for something that maybe got put in your grocery bag by mistake?"

"Where is all of this coming from?" Chase asked with a little chuckle. "Mena, I'm not a saint. I think this is the loss of blood talking."

"You make it look so easy ...I upset you this morning. I was being flip and stupid and ... you'd just come back from checking on this house you're giving someone for free ..."

Chase had to laugh just a little, although it was short lived. "Even your lips are white. Did I tell you that already? How are you feeling?"

Mena was resting her head back against the headrest. "Not good," she said softly. "I think I might —" She looked like she might throw up but then took a deep breath. "No. I'm not. It's good." She looked over at Chase again. "This really hurts. And you're just the most amazing human being I've ever met."

He smiled at her with a soft blush rising on his cheeks. "I didn't do anything. And you're delirious."

"You wouldn't know how to see someone hurting and not help. In some way. Could you?"

"I ... don't think I'd be happy being a person that didn't help others," he answered honestly.

"Am I taking advantage of that trait in you?"

"I'm not sure I understand that question," Chase said with a little smile.

"All of this with my grandfather's cottage. I thought that maybe we had connected somehow but ... the truth is ... you help everyone. Not just me. Not just my grandfather."

"Okay ... another sharp mental turn?" Chase asked. "Is me helping you now a bad thing?"

Mena shook her head, "Did I tell you that my hand really hurts. It's kind of moving up my arm."

"You know what? I'm sure you're going to need stitches. But once they fix you up, I'll take you home. I'll start a fire, we'll have a glass or two of wine, listen to some music and ... I think you'll feel better."

"I want to be ..." Mena looked at Chase but didn't finish her sentence.

"You want to be what?" Chase asked.

Mena shook her head, choosing to not say what she had been thinking. She didn't voice out loud that she wanted to be someone who could be worthy of Chase Harper. Instead she said, "That's an awful lot of blood."

CHAPTER THIRTEEN

Mena struggled to open her eyes, trying to remember having gone to bed. Her head was pounding, yet her body felt as if it were floating. She tried to roll over onto her side but wasn't successful. It seemed as if her body thought it was moving, but in reality she was perfectly still. With her eyes still closed she took in a deep breath and let it out slowly, frowning slightly when she heard unfamiliar noises around her. They definitely weren't the sound of a handsome builder doing construction nearby.

"Mena?"

She frowned again, hearing Chase's voice. Why did he sound so worried? What was wrong?

Again she struggled to open her eyes. When she did so things around her looked blurry, but she was almost positive she wasn't in her room in Chase's house. So where was she?

"Chase?" she asked softly, seeing the outline that was surely her roommate and landlord. "Where are we?"

She felt both of Chase's hands close over one of her own. "Oh Mena. You scared me," he said, the concern more than evident in his voice.

She squeezed her eyes closed tightly before opening them again, attempting to clear away the haze. Finally she could make out her friend's face.

"Chase, what's wrong?"

"You don't remember?" Chase asked.

"Remember what?" Mena looked around and her eyes widened. "Are we in a hospital?" She finally took in her surroundings and realized that she was in a hospital bed in what appeared to be a small emergency room. She quickly tried to sit up but the swimming in her head, combined with a pain that shot up her arm, kept her in place.

Chase moved a little closer to the bed, still holding her hand tightly. "You hurt your hand. The more it bled the dizzier you got and then you passed out. You didn't wake up, not even when I carried you in. You scared me to death." He lifted her good hand just enough to place a soft kiss upon it. "Please don't ever do that again."

Mena's eyes widened. "Oh Chase, I'm so sorry!"

"You don't have to be sorry. Not at all. I mean, it was a lot of blood."

Mena raised her bandaged hand. "Yeah. Now I remember. But it doesn't hurt as bad as it did before."

Chase gave her an emotional smile. "They put some shots of novocaine or something in there before they stitched it up. The doctor said it was really deep."

She searched his face. "I slept through stitches? Really?"

"You did. The doctor said they'd never had anybody do that," Chase answered, "But she did say you have a fever. That you probably had more going on than just the cut on your hand. I think all of that talk today was your brain saying that something just wasn't right. You have to take care of yourself and not ... pretend that you're okay."

"But I was okay. I ... thought. I mean, yeah there were some things that weren't perfect but ... "

"Mena, you passed out and didn't wake up when the nurse stuck four needles in your hand. That has to tell you something," Chase says softly.

"You need rest. No more physical or emotional multi-tasking. Okay?"

She offered him a little smile as she looked around. She caught the eye of a woman standing at a counter outside of Mena's room and groaned softly when the woman started walking toward the doorway.

"Well, I'm glad to see you awake. I'm Dr. Garnet. Can you tell me where you are?" The woman was now standing beside Mena's bed, taking her pulse. She looked to be in her thirties, reddish hair pulled back into a tight bun.

"It looks like I'm in a hospital," Mena answered. "But I don't know exactly where but only because I'm not that familiar with the area."

"How about your name?" the doctor asked while looking at the monitors.

"Mena Prescott."

"Can you tell me what happened?" Now the doctor was looking only at Mena.

"Yes. I accidentally leaned my hand against a piece of broken glass. I was feeling dizzy and I think that combined with the pain and the sight of all of the blood ... I passed out," Mena answered honestly.

"What's the last thing you remember?"

"I remember ...," Mena frowned for a few seconds as she thought. "Oh! I felt like I was going to throw up."

The doctor gave Chase a smile. "Was that today?"

Chase nodded.

"In Chase's truck. On the way here." Mena looked at Chase. "Did I throw up in your truck? Oh no. I'm so sorry!"

"No. You never actually threw up. It's okay,' Chase assured her.

"Okay well you have ten stitches in the palm of your hand," Dr. Garnet informed the patient. "We wrapped it up. You'll need to keep the bandages on for a few days. The nurse will give you instructions with your discharge papers. You're also going to get a Tetanus shot. But, also your heart rate and blood pressure were elevated when you came in. This could simply have been a result of the pain you were in. But Chase touched on the fact that you're going through what seems to be a stressful period in your life, and my advice to you would be to schedule an appointment with a therapist. I feel it would be best for you to have a professional help you work through everything that you're dealing with. See if that helps you physically as well."

"Dr. Garnet, I appreciate everything you've done, but I've really been alright. Today was just a ..." Mena laughed a little. "... it was just an accident. I think I must have been sick and not realized it. It made me a little dizzy and I stumbled, catching myself on the broken glass."

The doctor nodded. "Just the same, I think it would be beneficial for you to speak with someone. Okay, the nurse will be in with your discharge papers and I'm also going to send you home with a prescription for some pain medication. When what we gave you wears off you might start to get uncomfortable. But only take it if you need it. I'm only prescribing enough to last a week. Everything should be better by then. If it's not, I want you to come back so that we can reassess the situation. Otherwise, we'll see you in two weeks to remove the stitches. Alright? Do you have any questions?"

Mena shook her head. "Thank you doctor."

The doctor smiled and nodded before leaving the room.

"Why do I feel like I'm in trouble with the principal?" Mena whispered to Chase.

He smiled but it was obvious he was still concerned. "Don't make jokes. She took good care of you, Mena."

"And I guess I'm in trouble with the vice principal too."

Chase frowned.

"I'm just kidding," Mena assured him. "Thank you for helping me. Getting me here." Something else only then just hit her. "Did you call Gem or Tyler?"

Chase shook his head. "I ... didn't have any way to reach anyone. Your phone is locked."

Mena let out a sigh of relief. "Good. No, that's good. I'd hate to have my daughter worrying all the way up in Connecticut when it's nothing."

Again Chase frowned.

"I'm not saying it's nothing just ... nothing that would warrant an emergency trip to Delaware. That's all."

"You wouldn't say that if you'd see your hand," Chase said with a little shiver. "I've had guys hurt themselves on jobsites before but when they were checking out your hand ..." He shook his head. "I almost passed out right with you."

"I'm so sorry, Chase." Mena finally felt steady enough to get up. So she gathered her things and sat on the side of the bed waiting for the nurse, keeping her right arm bent against her chest. When the young woman came in, Mena listened as she went through the discharge instructions and the prescription. Then came the Tetanus shot that caused Mena to cry out.

After signing everything, Mena thanked the nurse and walked out with Chase at her side. He watched her as if he was afraid she could fall over at any moment.

The gray skies had now given way to night, leaving a starless, dark canvas above them as the pair made their way to the truck.

"So relatively speaking, where are we?" Mena asked as she let Chase help her into the truck.

"A little past Reeds Beach," he said somewhat quietly as he started the engine. He looked straight ahead for a second before turning to face Mena. "Did you mean those things you said?" he whispered.

"I ... don't really remember everything that I said. But if I hurt you ... I'm really sorry, Chase. I am. And I'm almost afraid to find out if I did or not."

Chase looked into her eyes for what seemed like forever. "I need to say something to you that ..." He sighed nervously. "I don't know if it's right or not. But ... I have to get it out."

Mena watched him and then nodded slightly. "Okay. Whatever you have to say, I probably ... deserve it."

He growled quietly. "So you started off the day asking who I was seeing that made me so happy. And then you ended the day by saying that I was only helping you because that's what I do. I help people. Not because I liked you or anything." He shook his head, reaching over and taking her good hand again. "Mena ... I'm happy when I'm around you, for just that reason. Any smile you see on my face is there because I'm with you. And I'd rebuild Chris' cottage or ... anything else I could do for you, because ... it keeps you here. Because it lets me be with you. So I know you're married and this will never be anything more than friends but ... for me ... on my end, Mena ... I think I have fallen in love with you. And if anything had happened to you today without me getting that said ... I'd have regretted it for the rest of my life. So ... please don't say anything. Just know that ... our relationship isn't one that I have with everybody in need. And I'm not smiling because I have some secret relationship going on when I'm not with you. It's you. It's all you."

Mena could only stare at him for a moment. She still felt weak and his words didn't do anything to help that feeling. She opened her mouth to try to find the right words but he quickly shook his head.

"No. Don't say anything. We can pretend like I never said it, if that's best. I just promised you honesty and ... there you go. So ... I'll stop at a pharmacy on the way home, and we can pick up dinner and then it's to bed with you and ... rest. For as long as you need it."

"Chase ...," Mena whispered.

"What would you like for dinner?" Chase asked, as the truck was now in motion. He was using the act of driving as a reason to not be able to look at her for the moment.

"Thank you. For everything you said. I'm ... so sorry for upsetting you."

"Upset me? No. No, you didn't upset me. I was worried about you. So if you're okay then I'm okay."

"Really?"

He nodded.

They drove another mile or two in silence, but finally Mena reached over, putting her hand on his arm.

"I heard you," she whispered. "And it means more than I can tell you right now."

He nodded again, still unable to turn and look at her.

"It wouldn't be right to talk to you before I talk to Tyler," she said, her words remaining a whisper.

He finally turned to glance at her face, lit softly by the dashboard lights. "It's okay." He took one hand off of the wheel and covered hers where it remained on his arm.

The events of the day added to the taking of her first dose of pain medication caused Mena to sleep deeply that night. Chase had served her dinner in bed and the food had barely been touched before she drifted off. He had been sitting in a chair that he'd pulled closer to the bed, even though she'd assured him she would be fine. So it must have been him that removed her plate from the bed and put it on the bedside table. And now, as Mena's eyes opened, she expected to still see him in that chair. But it was empty as it sat in a pool of sunlight that now danced throughout the room. Mena reached over and picked up her phone, going through her messages.

She sent 'I love you. I hope today is a good day!' to Gemma along with a picture of the sun coming in the door from the balcony.

She had a text from Liz, asking how she was feeling, which led Mena to believe that she had more than likely spoken to Chase at some point since the 'incident'. She responded to her friend with, 'Doing good. Thanks. Just a little sore. Great night's sleep!'

Another text from Liz popped up pretty quickly. 'Can I come see you today, since I doubt you'll be coming to the store?'

Mena smiled. She didn't take for granted the fact that someone truly cared for her. But she still didn't think she'd be good company. 'I'm probably going to stay in bed today and sleep. Tomorrow?'

Liz's response was another quick one 'Tomorrow it is. Get some rest. Let me know if you need anything.'

Then, as she was reaching to sit her phone back down she saw that a new call was coming in. From Tyler. She seriously considered not answering, but she wanted to be a better person than one who would do that. Today was as good a day as any to start. So she put the phone to her ear.

"Hello?"

"Hey," Tyler answered. "Are you busy?"

"Actually I'm still in bed."

"Really? You don't usually sleep in this late."

"I wasn't feeling good last night, so I took some medicine. I think it knocked me out," Mena answered, feeling that it was enough of the truth.

"Mena," Tyler sighed. "Are we ever going to talk again? Each day that passes that I don't hear from you ... I'm starting to worry that ... you may have left for good. Did you? Did you ... leave me?"

Mena closed her eyes, blocking out the beautiful visions of the sun and the blue sky stretching out over the water. "Tyler, I wouldn't do that. I wouldn't end our marriage with ... silence. Or running away. I think you know me well enough to know that's now how I would do it. We both deserve better than that."

There was silence for a moment before Tyler spoke again. "But you're going to end it. Aren't you?" he whispered. "I can't imagine that being away from me at your grandfather's cottage all this time is making you fall in love with me again."

This wasn't the time or place that Mena wanted to have this conversation, but if Tyler was ready then she owed him an honest response. "I wish I could say that it was making things seem better, but it's not, Tyler. I'm sorry," she said softly.

"There's nothing I can do?" Tyler asked. "Nothing that will change your mind? We can go away. The two of us. Work on putting things back together. Talk about how we both feel."

"I don't want either of us to be fooled by beautiful surroundings. It would all still be there, waiting for us when we got back home. And Tyler, at the core, it isn't Nikki ... it's the dishonesty. It's that you were in my life and didn't tell me what you were doing. You didn't work with me on what might have been wrong to cause you to have an affair. You broke our trust, Tyler. And I've looked at it from every angle but ... that's the part I don't see us fixing."

"Baby, I can't take this. You've been my life for so long. And now to know that you hate me—"

"No," Mena interrupted. "That's just it, Tyler. I have worked on that part of our problem and ... I don't hate you. Sincerely, there is no hate. Because I've realized that I must have played some part in the road our relationship took. And no matter what happens, I don't want us to hate each other. For our own mental health, but also, for Gemma. She doesn't deserve to have her life ripped apart because of what's happened with you and me."

"I don't want to hurt her," Tyler said quietly. "I didn't want to hurt you," he added.

"Tyler, how about if I come back to Connecticut in a few days and we can talk this all out. Alright? With love and with honesty. What we had deserves that. Don't you think?"

"Really?"

"Really. And maybe after we talk we can go have dinner with Gem."

"Yeah," Tyler whispered, his voice breaking. "It'll be good to see you again."

"You too, Ty. I'll let you know when I'm coming. Bye." And she disconnected the call, sighing deeply. She had little time to digest the unspoken decision she had just made due to a knock on the bedroom door. "Yeah?"

"Can I come in?" came Chase's voice through the door.

"Yes. Of course."

She watched the door open slowly and smiled when he appeared.

"I thought I heard your voice," Chase said. "So I wanted to check on you. How are you feeling this morning?"

She gave him a smile, scooting herself up to a sitting position. "Better. Thank you. My head is a little groggy and my arm is starting to throb a bit, but other than that I'm right as rain. Pretty normal." She looked at his face, where she was sure she still saw concern. "I'm really sorry, Chase. For putting you through all of that. It really does seem like a dream."

"But you're going to do what the doctor said, right?"

"Yes. Absolutely. Pain medication as needed. Keeping it dry and covered ..."

"What about the part about finding a therapist. Have somebody help you work things out?" he asked hesitantly.

Mena nodded. "I am. I promise. But before I do that, I ... wanted to tell you something."

Chase stood motionless near the doorway, only nodding slightly.

"I just spoke with Tyler. I told him that I'll be home this week," she said gently.

"Oh," Chase whispered, nodding yet again. "Oh ..."

She quickly smiled. "No. It's not like that. It's not fair that I hide down here. He deserves to hear my honest feelings. My decision. He knows that's what we're doing. That it's why we're meeting."

"You told him that you want a divorce?" Chase asked, doing his best not to smile.

"I told him that I don't see our relationship being put back together as anything other than friends. But he deserves to hear that face to face. I can't take the coward's way out. Hide behind a lawyer's delivery to his doorstep."

Chase walked over to the bed and sat down gently at the end, turning to look at her. "Will you ... come back?" he asked softly.

"I'd like to. If that's okay with you."

"Yes. Of course," he stammered. "You're sure? I don't want to have ... pushed you. With what I said last night."

"Chase, this has nothing to do with you," Mena said. "You might have helped me find the courage to voice my true feelings, but ... I left Connecticut with the same thoughts and feelings that I have now. Maybe I go back and forth on how I feel about Tyler, but it's the trust. Once someone has lied in such a big way. Betrayed you. You can't fix that. Because regardless of what they say or do ... how do you believe it? How do you learn to trust again?"

Chase nodded. "I understand," he whispered. "I'm sorry."

She smiled. "You're sorry? Don't be. You're an honest man, Chase. If anything, you're what showed me that there are other choices in life. That not all men are like Tyler."

He returned the smile and got up off of the bed. "Well I actually didn't know you were talking to Tyler. But when I heard that you were awake I wanted you to see what you've missed. Come here." He walked to the front window, reaching his hand back for her.

Mena climbed out of the covers and walked over to Chase. She took his hand with her good one, walking the last few steps at his side.

"Check it out," Chase said, the smile still on his face.

Mena looked toward the cottage and saw the amount of work that had been done while she slept under the blanket of her pain medication. "Chase! It's really happening!"

The ground around the cottage had been trenched out, with jacks and support beams now placed beneath the structure.

"It's really happening," Chase said. "Are you happy?"

She nodded, tears in her eyes. "You made this happen. This is all because of you. Thank you," she said softly, as she turned to look at him.

"You're very welcome. I love being a part of something that makes you happy. And if you want to repay the favor, why don't you get back in bed for today. I'd feel better if you'd just rest. For a day at least."

Mena looked back at the cottage, leaning against Chase's arm. "How about if I promise to take it easy. I'll shower and maybe just curl up on the couch? Oh! I talked to Liz. She wanted to stop by. I told her maybe tomorrow would be better. Is that alright?"

"Yeah. Of course. But you'll rest today?"

Mena smiled. "Yes sir."

He looked at her, smiling, as if there was so much he wanted to say. But he just kissed her on the top of her head and took a step back. "While you're in the shower—"

"Yes?" Mena asked, giggling.

"No. No. That's not ... No," Chase said. "While you're in the shower, could I make you something for lunch? Are you hungry? You should eat if you'll be taking another of your pills."

Mena enjoyed the slight blush on Chase's cheeks. "I don't want you to go to any trouble. I'll just make some toast or a sandwich or something. But I won't be long. I'll be right down."

"Okay," Chase said, grinning. "Seriously though, if you start to feel dizzy or something, sit down right away. I don't want you to fall and hit your head."

"I will. Promise."

"Okay then ... I'll see you downstairs."

"See you downstairs," Mena repeated.

CHAPTER FOURTEEN

Mena had taken her orders from both the doctor and Chase more seriously than she'd intended. After she'd showered, she ended up climbing back into bed. She was checked on by Chase several times and eventually went downstairs for dinner. He gave her the classic 'I'm sick' meal of soup and a grilled cheese sandwich. And as with anything he cooked for her, it was delicious. Afterwards, Chase put on more of his father's records while Mena curled up on the couch, a blanket over her and a pillow beneath her head.

She hadn't realized she'd fallen asleep until she heard Liz's quiet voice.

"Maybe I should come back later. I knew this was too early."

"She'll be waking up soon," Chase whispered. "Can I get you anything?"

"Maybe just some juice?" Liz asked as she sat down on the end of the couch.

Mena opened her eyes and smiled. "Hi Liz. Sorry. I'm under orders to not do anything so I've just kind of been sleeping on and off all day."

"No problem with me," Liz assured her. "I'm just glad to see that you're alive and kicking. When Chase called me the other night he scared the shit out of me."

Mena looked toward the kitchen, catching Chase's eye. "You called her the other night?"

"I just ... wanted to talk to somebody," Chase explained.

"No, it's okay. I'm sorry to have worried both of you. I just mean ... is it tomorrow?"

Liz smiled, rubbing Mena's leg. "Well, technically they call it today. And hey, I finally got my behind out here to see your place."

Mena nodded, but she was looking at Chase who was now bringing in Liz's glass of orange juice. "Did I sleep down here all night?"

"I didn't want to wake you. I slept in the chair in case you needed anything."

"Thank you," Mena said softly.

He gave her a nod while Liz took the glass of juice.

"I think that cottage has seen better days," Liz said as she looked out the window.

Mena laughed. "It's being raised. Today they got everything put in place. The supports. The jacks. I mean ... yesterday ... This is going to be so exciting. I hope they don't do too much while I'm gone. I want to see it actually go up in the air."

"You're leaving?" Liz asked with a little pout. "When? Why?"

Chase had returned to the kitchen and now came back, holding out a glass of water toward Mena. "Hydrate," he said softly before leaving the two women to talk.

"I'm going to talk to Tyler. In person," Mena said.

Liz nodded slowly.

"What?" Mena asked. "You don't think I should?"

A small smile took up residence on Liz's lips. "I want you to do whatever makes you happy. I'm just ... worried about you, I guess. Doing that alone. Especially with your hand and everything."

Mena reached and patted Liz's arm. "Oh I'll be fine. I promise."

The two women sat on the couch, talking quietly for almost an hour before Liz reached out her hand. "I think you need some fresh air. Why don't we take a little walk? We won't have too many more of these warm, gorgeous days."

Chase, who had been trying to give the women their privacy, jumped in with, "Liz, I think she should just stay where she is."

"We're not going to walk to Maryland, Chase. Just to the water and back. It'll do her good."

"I'll be okay, Chase," Mena assured him. "And if I start not feeling good I'll turn right back around."

"Really? Promise?"

"Nothing but truth, right?"

Chase nodded. "Okay then."

"Wow, you're like a warden, " Liz laughed.

Before going outside, Mena grabbed her sweater, laying it over her shoulders as the two women made their way to the beach.

"Just hearing the waves is such good medicine," Mena said, closing her eyes. The air was warm but was giving glimpses of the chill that October started to usher in after a beautiful September. Mena held her sweater around her a little tighter. "It's really nice that you stopped by today, Liz. You're a good friend," she said as they both looked out at the water. "Do you remember that day in your shop that you said something about maybe my grandfather knew that I was going through something and needed this cottage? This ... refuge ... The way it had been for him?"

Liz nodded. "Are you feeling that way now too?"

"I really am. I've talked to Chase so much about Christopher and his life down here. He loved my grandmother, but in this cottage ... on this beach ... it's where he was completely happy. He was at peace."

"And is Brandford bringing you peace too?" Liz asked.

"It is. My world has become so small. And if that was the way it was in Connecticut ... I'd be going crazy. It would be suffocating. I'd need to be occupied. Busy. To not be thinking about Tyler or my life or what I was going to do. But here ... there are actually times where there is absolutely nothing on my mind. And it's so comfortable. I mean yesterday I literally did nothing and ..."

"There's no noise anymore," Liz asked.

"No. There's no underlying noise. I've actually been able to relax. Even with ... whatever happened the other day. But today I feel like ... you know when somebody's been working on a car and they get in to start it up finally and it blows out this black smoke for just a second and then it's gone? Then it's clear?"

"Blowing out the carbon?" Liz asked.

Mena laughed quietly. "Yes. Blowing out the carbon." She put her good arm through Liz's as they walked slowly. "You know, last night Chase was playing some of his father's records. He has this amazing vinyl collection that I have loved looking through. But Chase started with the album that was already on the turntable, and put the needle down ... Do you know the song 'Lowdown'? Boz Scaggs?"

Liz nodded. "Yeah, I think so."

"My life is so tied to music. Musical memories. And this song had always made me ... kind of sad. It was so tied to me being young. Car rides with my family. But I've listened to it here and ... it sounded so good. And ... new. I don't know how to explain it. But it was like I was making these brand new memories. Like my laptop if it was suddenly wiped clean. I didn't listen to the song thinking about how much I miss the way my family used to be. Or how ... maybe I played it at my house while I was fixing dinner for Tyler and Gemma. I'm sure I sound like I'm ..."

"Healing?" Liz asked. "Because to me it sounds like you're finally healing. Maybe even from things long before your husband's affair."

"Healing," Mena repeated, nodding. "Yes. Exactly. Wounds are closing ... some after decades ... And it's not just because I'm thinking about redoing the cottage so it's blocking everything else out. It's just ..." She takes in a deep breath and lets it out slowly. "everything is just drifting away ..." She turned to face her friend. "And ... I'm going back home."

"I have to say that when you mentioned that ... I didn't see that one coming."

"It's time. I'm going to finally say the D word out loud to Tyler. Start figuring out our future. Separate, but together for Gem. It's not like I've been avoiding the topic. It's more like my mind and my heart have just ... known the answer. All along. I was just too afraid to actually accept it. But he called yesterday morning and it just seemed right. For honesty and ... healing."

Liz gave her a smile and then leaned in to hug her tight, careful not to hurt her. "I'm so proud of you. And I hope that doesn't sound condescending. But ... this is the right decision." She motioned back toward the way they'd come. "And maybe after you take care of things you could ... I don't know ... maybe come back and give Chase a chance. A real chance. I can see how much he cares for you. It's in his eyes when he looks at you."

"Chase and I are friends," Mena said. "But ... he has really opened up since we were in the hospital. He's been so good about everything. I couldn't ask for a better friend."

"Yeah. Of course you are friends. But I think if you weren't married, you might admit that you feel more for him than just friendship."

Mena smiled. "I'm trying to … do things the right way. Talking to Tyler before I invite anything else in. But if I wasn't married … do you think that would make Chase happy?"

Liz nodded. "I've never seen him like this. The way he is with you. He keeps so much to himself. Hiding in his work and that house. It makes me so mad."

"That he hides?"

"That people make him think he has to hide! Some people just can't let shit go, you know? But you. You're all about honesty. You keep pushing that and to know that he's finally opened up to somebody … Somebody as special as you … You've made the people that love him so happy, Mena."

Mena was sure she looked as lost as she felt. "Liz, I have no idea what you're talking about."

"His grandfather. I thought he told you."

"Oh! Yes. About him dying."

Liz nodded.

"He fell and hit his head. Why would people treat Chase differently because of that? His whole life is about taking care of others. Was he supposed to have had the medical training at that age to save the man's life?"

Liz was quiet. She hesitated before forcing a smile and saying, "Right."

"Liz? What am I missing?" Mena asked. "What's the look on your face about?"

"Oh nothing," Liz answered quickly. "We should probably get back. Chase is going to think I kidnapped you. I was under strict orders to not take you far."

Mena reached out and put her hand on the other woman's arm. "Liz. Please,"

"Mena, I'm sorry. I shouldn't have said anything. I don't want to … I can't believe I shot off my mouth. Just forget I said anything."

"How can I just forget?" Mena asked. "Maybe it's still because I'm a little foggy from my medication but … the pieces aren't going together. I saw the house Chase was building for free for that family. Why would people treat him like shit because his grandfather died decades ago? You're not making any sense."

Liz walked a few steps away from Mena, the breeze feeling like it was going through her. She turned to face her friend. "He killed his grandfather." She shrugged sadly. "Okay? He killed him. But he was just a boy, Mena ..."

Any other words Liz said didn't penetrate Mena's brain. She thought of Chase's face when he told her the story of his grandfather dying. He was so emotional. He seemed so open. So honest. But he wasn't. He left out that one piece of the story. That critical detail. After their promises of no more lies to each other. No more strategic stringing together of words to avoid the truth. She had almost believed him. She could feel it happening again. Her head was swimming.

"Mena? Please don't —"

Mena waved off whatever words might be coming next as she started back for the house. She felt as if each step was taken in a dream, filled with blinding fog. She could feel the tears hit her cheeks, turning cold as soon as the air hit their trail across her skin. She kept her head down as she made her way to the stairs leading to Chase's front door. She could hear him call to her from the direction of the cottage but she didn't look around. Instead she went straight up to her room and closed the door. She felt like the very ground beneath her feet was crumbling away. Soon she would be in a freefall, with no hope of getting her footing again.

A few moments later she heard a car door close. She walked over to the front window and parted the curtains enough to see that Liz was now in her car, speaking to Chase through her open window. In a second it was as if they both sensed her standing there, each turning their eyes to the bedroom window. She quickly stepped back, out of their view. She wiped her face and pushed her hair back, trying to calm down and stop the shaking that was taking over her entire body.

The only thing she could think of doing to keep from collapsing was to pack. After all, she was already planning on going home to talk to Tyler. Why not get a jump on the task of getting everything back into her suitcase? Just as Chase had not been a factor in Mena deciding to ask for a divorce, his actions now wouldn't change that decision. Regardless of what her future held, it was not going to be a future where she lived as Tyler Prescott's wife.

She took her suitcase out of the closet and began to take her clothes out of the drawers and off of the hangers. Her heart seemed to stop when she heard Chase's footsteps on the stairs.

His knock on her door seemed to echo straight through to her soul.

"Mena?" he called through softly. "We need to talk. What Liz said to you ... "

She stood frozen in place as he knocked again.

"Can I just explain?" he asked, his voice pleading with her.

She knew that she had to confront him so she gathered her strength and finally opened the door. "Did you do it?" she whispered. "Is that what happened? Not the story you told me? I can't believe I believed you. Completely. Well ... you did a good job, Chase. You'll make a great writer."

"Mena, I can explain," he said, looking almost as upset as she felt.

"It's just ... yes or no ...," she said, her words still a softly spoken whisper, her eyes unable to meet his. "It's just 'I killed a man' or 'I didn't kill a man'."

"What I told you was the truth."

"So Liz was lying?"

"No, but it's not that black and white—"

"You either killed a man or you didn't," Mena said, her voice now raised. When she finally brought her eyes up to look into his she quietly said, "You promised that you wouldn't lie to me again. No more secrets. I would think that would especially apply to something this big. My parents must have known. They didn't think your grandfather had a heart attack, because they knew that you'd killed him. That's why they didn't bring us down here anymore."

Chase looked behind her and saw her open suitcase on the bed. "Mena please. Can we just talk? Don't you know me well enough to know what I am and am not capable of? I've told you more than I've ever told anyone else. Ever."

"Except that one little thing," Mena whispered. "I can't do this with you, Chase. My head just ... can't." She wiped at the tears on her cheeks. "You said that I could trust you," she said so softly. "And I believed you. And it hurts. It hurts too much right now. I'm sorry."

"And just like that what we might have had is over? You're leaving? Come on, Mena!" Chase pleaded. "You know how I feel about you. Don't go."

Mena was quiet for a moment but then answered. "I was going home anyway. I told you that. I just ... figured there's no use in waiting anymore.

I'll just leave tonight."

"Not like this. Mena please. Please don't go." He reached out to touch her arm but she flinched and almost involuntarily took a quick step back. The pain that small movement caused him was evident in his eyes. He finally just nodded and turned, slowly leaving the room, and closing the door behind him.

Mena stood at the door, her hand against it. She wanted to go after him, but she couldn't. He'd taken a life and then lied to her about it. It was something she couldn't deal with tonight. Sadly, Tyler seemed like the safer place to be.

But her decision didn't seem to matter when she soon heard Chase's truck start and drive off. It was then that the tears started to fall once again.

With her suitcases packed back up, Mena dragged everything out to her car. One suitcase at a time, pulled in one hand. She opened the back door and pushed them onto the seat. Headlights suddenly lit her up as a car turned onto the road. It pulled up next to Mena, letting her see that it was Liz.

"Mena, I just couldn't let you go home like this. I have to try to fix what I've done," Liz said, clearly still upset. "Where's Chase?"

Mena shrugged. "He left not long after you."

"Okay, you need to hear the whole story."

Mena offered her friend a tired smile. "Liz, this isn't your fault."

"Mena, stop." Liz got out of the car and put her hand on Mena's arm, leading her to the chairs where Mena had sat so many times watching the work being done on the cottage. When they were both sitting, Liz began talking. "After what I said to you, I could tell that you all of a sudden pictured Chase as this mass murderer. And he didn't do anything wrong–"

"Liz, you don't have to do this. Chase killed a man. That's something to process. And the fact that he hid that from me ... Knowing that honesty was all I asked from him ..."

"Look. I know you have things that you have to take care of at home. But Chase didn't suddenly turn into a different person. He's the same person that you've known since you got here. The same man that could barely breathe while he sat next to your hospital bed. Doesn't he deserve the right to explain everything to you?"

"Of course he had that right, Liz. But he chose to make up a story instead," Mena said sadly.

"You need to come back here and work things out. Really talk to him. Give him a real shot. Not too many people do. It would just break my heart if his worst fear came true."

"His worst fear?"

"He said that when people found out what happened to him ... they changed. He's lost friends ... It's why he doesn't date. He never puts himself out there. He won't even have his name anywhere with this house. He has a post office box so that mail isn't delivered here with his name on it."

"Whatever happened was decades ago ...," Mena said softly.

"But that didn't matter to you, did it?" Liz whispered. "And it doesn't matter to some other people either."

"My reaction was because he lied to me," Mena pointed out quickly.

"Was it really? Honestly?" Liz looked over at her friend. "Do you want to know what happened?"

"Don't you think that Chase should tell me if he wants me to know?" Mena asked quietly.

"He knows your reaction. I doubt he's going to share the most painful thing from his life with you."

"Did he ask you to tell me?" Mena asked. The thought just coming to her mind.

Liz shook her head. "He'd never do that."

After a moment Mena nodded. "If you want to tell me ..."

Liz took a deep breath before starting with, "Well I think you know when it happened. You and your family were staying at the cottage that night."

Again Mena nodded.

"Well ... Henry Kash ... Chase's grandfather on his mother's side, was drunk. That wasn't a rare thing. It also wasn't rare to have Henry picking a fight with Steven."

"For what? From everything Chase has said, his father was a kind man ...," Mena said.

"He was," Liz answered with a nod. "But that didn't matter to Henry. I think his favorite thing to throw at Steven was that he couldn't provide for his family. That no man should have to have his father-in-law bail him out. How Chase's mother should have never married him. Stuff like that. It got to Steven. He worked for some kind of non profit, helping people. Maybe not the most lucrative job for a married man with two kids, but he was passionate about using his life to help others. To be of service to his neighbors. His community. Chase's mother never got involved when these fights would happen. She didn't disagree with her father or defend her husband. She'd just take her daughter and leave the room. Or sometimes the house. Apparently that's what she did on that night. They went to a movie or something. Henry gave them the money. So the fact that he gave them movie or dinner money or whatever just kicked the fight up a notch. Henry was physically poking Steven, shoving him so hard that he had started to stumble backwards. Which made Henry laugh. Chase told the police that his father never fought back. That he'd never seen his father even raise his voice to another person, much less react to someone in anger. But Chase ... he loved Steven with all of his heart. And I guess on that particular night he'd had enough of watching his precious father be belittled and abused by this ... drunk. So Chase stepped in between them and gave his grandfather a shove backwards. I guess because he was so drunk he lost his balance and fell. He struck his head on the corner of a table and ... died."

The two women sat in silence as that last word seemed to hang in the cold air around them.

"Steven called the police and even though he said it was an accident, they still took both Steven and Chase in for questioning. Since Chase was the one that physically did the pushing, they kept him longer."

"But he was just a boy," Mena whispered.

"I guess they had to make sure he wasn't a boy that committed murder and was covering it up with his father's help," Liz said with a little shrug. She turned to look at Mena. "That's your murderer. A boy that defended his father against a drunk and a bully. He has so much trouble forgiving himself, even after all of this time. I think it was easier when Steven was alive but now ... Chase has too much quiet time that is perfect for helping that guilt to fester. I know it's part of why he pushes himself to help as many people as he physically can. Hoping it makes up for taking a life."

Mena wiped tears from her cheeks, "Liz, I didn't know."

"But in your heart ... shouldn't you have known? Do you really think a man like Chase could be that good at hiding a dark soul? He's as good as they come, Mena. Don't hurt him. So many other people already have. He doesn't deserve it."

"I'm sorry, Liz," Mena whispered. "I'll talk to him. I promise."

Liz tilted her head just a little. "Really? You will?"

Mena nodded. "I'll wait for him to get back. I won't leave until we get a chance to talk."

Liz's face broke into a smile as she threw her arms around Mena, almost causing her chair to tip over. Both women had a much needed laugh for a moment before they stood, embracing again.

"Be careful driving home," Mena said, squeezing Liz's hand.

"I will. Talk soon?"

"Of course. And thank you so much, Liz."

"That's what friends are for," she answered, starting up her car. "Bye, hon."

Mena waved as the woman's car pulled away. She took out her phone and tried Chase's number, but there was no answer. It went straight to voicemail. She locked up her car and went back inside, curling up on the couch, pulling the blanket that still laid on the cushions over her lap. As she sat there, her conversation with Liz rolling over and over in her head, she saw Chase's phone sitting on the counter. That explained him not picking up the phone. At least she hoped it did. The rest could be explained as soon as he was back home.

She waited for hours for Chase to return, until finally she couldn't stay awake any longer. She drifted off into a sleep full of fitful dreams of the secrets held within this home's walls.

CHAPTER FIFTEEN

The sun was just rising over the water when Mena awoke. It took her a moment to remember the events of the night before, but as soon as they took shape in her mind she hurried to the front windows. She leaned closer in hopes of seeing Chase's truck parked in its usual spot. But her heart sank when she saw that her car was the only one on the street.

She had already let Gemma know that she was leaving for home this morning and if she were honest with herself, her belief that everything could be made right with Chase so easily was waning. So she reluctantly got out a piece of paper to leave a note.

Chase,

I'm sorry that I didn't hear you out last night when you tried to explain. As you know I had already made plans to return home, but hopefully we can clear the air when we see each other again.

Mena

She purposely took her time getting ready to leave, hoping Chase would walk in at any moment. But an hour had passed and she knew she had to get on the road. She could only handle one thing at a time. And today was the day she wanted to finally settle things with Tyler. She had to go while she was still committed to the decision. It would be too easy to stay at

Brandford Beach and hide from the situation. Or find another place to hide from both situations.

As she drove away from the beach her eyes searched every inch of the road for that familiar pickup truck. Where had he stayed all night? How deeply must she have hurt him to have him avoid coming back to his own home just to keep from having to see her?

The music that she played on the way back to Connecticut had a different feel than when she was driving south almost two weeks ago. She may have rid herself of the demons of childhood memories, but now she couldn't stop the thoughts of Chase. The memories she had made since arriving in Brandford. How had her life and feelings been able to change so quickly?

She had tried to call Chase a few more times during the drive but they continued to go straight to voicemail. She couldn't imagine how the splintering of a friendship that she'd only had for such a short time could cause her so much pain. But it did. Especially knowing the pain she had caused Chase. A man that had been nothing but kind to her.

It was almost three o'clock before she pulled into the familiar driveway of the home she'd shared with her husband for the last fifteen years of their marriage. The home was beautiful. Larger and more comfortable than anything at Brandford Beach. So why did she miss Christopher's cottage as she sat in her car, postponing getting out as long as she could? But when she saw Tyler standing in the doorway she knew the time had come. She turned off the engine, Carly Simon's 'Coming Around Again' continuing to play until the driver's side door opened.

Once Mena was out of the car Tyler opened the front door and walked outside, as if he had been waiting to see if she was actually going to stay. Or maybe she'd put her car in reverse and leave again. He approached her, giving her an awkward hug before taking a step back.

"Can I get your bags?" he asked. Then he looked down at her bandaged hand. "What happened?"

Mena shook her head. "Just a little accident. I got a few stitches. But if you want to get my bags, they'd probably get in a lot faster than if I pulled them out one by one. Thank you. Did Gemma get back to you about dinner?"

"Yes. But she said she'd rather come here. A friend was driving home so she was going to catch a ride with her. She said she'd be here around five," Tyler answered as he pulled the two suitcases off of the rear seat of the car. "I've really missed you," he said quietly as they walked together to the front door, following her inside. "I hope it's okay that I say that." He sat her bags down in the foyer and said, "I'm sorry the house isn't like you always kept it. I tried to keep up on things but—"

"The house looks fine, Ty," Mena said softly. "Can we go sit down and talk? I think we just need to rip this bandaid off so that we can both relax a little."

There was pain in his eyes as he nodded. He may have already known how Mena was feeling, but that didn't mean this would hurt any less.

They walked to the family room and after getting into the routine of having music playing at the beach house, she walked over to their stereo. She looked through their cd collection and decided on Eric Clapton's *Slowhand*.

"I've realized I wanted to get some of my favorite albums on vinyl again," Mena said as she sat down on the couch, turning slightly to face Tyler. "I've lost or given away so many records over the years ..."

"Is that what you really want to start with? Cds vs vinyl?" Tyler asked.

"No. Sorry," Mena said before, "Ty, I've taken the time since I've left to do some much needed thinking. About us. About my grandfather. About the future."

"Mena, I know what you said on the phone, but please just give me a chance to show you that I—"

"Tyler, look at me," Mena said, reaching for his hand. "I'm not angry anymore, or hurt. I'm not dissolving into tears. I forgive you. I meant what I said on the phone. I do."

He looked into her eyes and she knew that she still saw hope in his.

She shook her head slightly. "I forgive you Ty," she said again. "But ... I don't want to be your wife anymore. I'm sorry."

Tyler's whole body seemed to slump as he processed her crushing words.

"Tyler, listen to me. If I had truly been the person that you wanted, you wouldn't have had to go searching for more. And that's not the lead in to dragging out an old argument. I say that with nothing but honesty and logic. A happy man doesn't need a mistress."

"But Me, if you just let me—"

"You don't have to do anything, Ty," Mena said softly. "I want us to stay friends. I want the three of us to still be able to get together for the big moments in Gemma's life. And most of all, I sincerely want you to be happy, Ty."

"What if I need to have you to be happy?" he whispered.

"I think that right now, you think that's what you're supposed to say," Mena said, squeezing his hand before letting go. "I had to be sad if I was a good wife. And you have to want me back to be a good husband. But that's not true, Ty. It's okay for you to think that just maybe the whole Nikki thing was your way of screaming inside that you wanted more. Now's the time to have more! To revisit your decisions and see which one you made that resulted in your heading down the wrong path. You're still young enough to change your course."

"You mean like living out my dream of being a rock star?" Tyler asked, trying to smile.

"I've heard you sing so ... maybe not that one," Mena said, causing them both to laugh for just a second.

"So ... what about you?" Tyler then asked. "I'm guessing ... you found something you want for your new life? I have no right to get angry if you did the same thing to me that I did to you ..."

"You mean did I have an affair?"

Tyler nodded slightly.

"No, Ty. I swear to you that I didn't do that. I wouldn't do that to you. But I did realize that my grandfather knew exactly what he was doing when he left me his cottage. A decision that had just seemed so random to me at the time, turned out to make perfect sense. Somehow he gave me what I needed at the exact time I needed it most."

"I don't understand," Tyler whispered.

"Being down there I was forced to really look at my family ... my memories ... to forgive myself for the distance I put between us. But also own my part in how things got to where they are."

"You and me?"

She shook her head. "No. My parents. My brother and sister. And my grandparents. I've heard stories of how happy Christopher was. And most importantly ... how much he always loved me. I didn't realize how much I needed to know that. How much I needed to let go of the past and the expectations I put on other people. To love people for who they are. And to not only feel that love when they're gone."

Tyler sighed. "Why can't I fit into these realizations? Why do we have to be done just because you ... want to make amends with your family? Can't we make amends too?"

"I do include you in that, Ty," Mena said. "I love you for who you are. Who am I to demand that you be perfect when I'm so imperfect myself? Realizing that we're not meant to be husband and wife, doesn't mean that I'm going to carry around some martyr-like burden of being a victim. I want to let go of all things that weighed me down with so much sadness over the summer, and for so many years of my life."

Tyler's eyes were filled with tears. "I don't want to not be your husband, Me," he whispered.

"I think you're going to see that everything is going to be alright, Tyler. I promise you."

"I don't want you to leave."

"I'm not leaving your life. Just ... this house," Mena said. "Ty, we start making new memories right now. You and me. So ... let's make our first one a good one. Let's start on dinner. We can talk. Work things out so that we can talk to Gemma when she gets here. So that she can see that we're going to be alright."

Tyler reached out and squeezed her hand. "Will you help me? If I make a misstep or two?"

"I'll be the best friend you've ever had, Ty." Mena leaned over to hug her soon to be ex husband, then she got up off of the couch and changed the cd to another track before dancing her way into the kitchen. She was doing her best to come off as feeling light and carefree with her decisions. And maybe if it hadn't been for what happened with Chase, she would be. But for now she'd fake it until it was real. This was the harder of the wounds to heal. And she had to believe that Chase would forgive her as she had forgiven Tyler.

The small family had done their best to come together for that dinner and start writing their next chapter. It had gone as well as could have been expected, and Mena was glad that Tyler had seemed to be putting Gemma's feelings before his own. Promising her that they would always be a family and together for her whenever she needed them. There had been laughter and tears, and when the sun rose the next morning, there were goodbyes.

Tyler stood in the doorway, waving, as mother and daughter set out as they'd done almost two weeks earlier. Music played softly from the radio as they started their journey back to Gemma's school. As she drove, Mena reached over and let her bandaged hand rest on her daughter's knee.

"Are you okay, sweetheart?" she asked gently.

Gemma didn't answer for a moment but then nodded. "I guess it's just weird. I mean I knew it was coming. We've talked about it. And it's not even like I didn't want you to do what you needed to do to be happy. But … I guess the reality is sinking in. Like I won't go back to that house to be with my family for Thanksgiving or Christmas …"

Mena's heart broke as she saw the tears slide down her daughter's cheek. She couldn't hold back her own any longer. "Gem, your father and I are okay. We talked for so many hours last night. And we're going to do everything with only one purpose in mind, and that's to make sure that you're okay. I promise you. So when Thanksgiving comes around, you're going to see your family. Maybe it won't be like other years but … you'll see your Mom and Dad."

"Is Daddy keeping the house?" Gemma asked.

"That's up to him. If he wants to. The next time you talk to him let him know your thoughts. Tell him what you're hoping he does."

"But he hurt you, Mom," she whispered. "I feel … weird. Pretending it's fine. What he did."

Mena shook her head. "Baby girl, I am fine. I really am. I've done so much soul searching over these past weeks that I just … I can't even tell you how at peace I feel with my decision. And you and your father having a great relationship will only add to that peace."

"Really?"

"One hundred percent. The three of us are each starting on a new chapter in our lives, but we'll be coming back together to share our progress and our stories."

"I love you Mom," Gemma said, wiping away her tears. "Where are you going to stay?"

"Well for right now I'm going to head back to the beach and … handle things there. … Get things settled for the winter. After that, who knows. Maybe I'll stay with your grandparents," she said with a wide eyed expression that made them both laugh. When they stopped, she added, "But whatever plans I make, you will always be the first to know. And don't forget that next summer we're going to be staying in our own, newly renovated beach house for as long as your schedule allows."

"I can't wait, Mom," Gemma answered. "I'll be glad to get the holidays and things over with and by then ... maybe we'll all be happy."

"I think we will be!"

As Mena drove down 95 through Pennsylvania she started seeing the signs for West Chester. She was in a hurry to get back to Brandford to try and apologize to Chase, but being this close to her parents, she knew she had to stop. She had to prove to herself that she had truly grown as a person over these last two weeks. That she did clearly see the road she wanted to walk as she went into an unknown future. So at the last minute she put on her turn signal and eased off of the highway, to make her way to the home that she left almost two decades before.

It took almost twenty minutes to get to the driveway that led back to the farmhouse style home that her parents bought shortly after their wedding. She could only imagine the reception that she would get, if they were even home. But if they weren't she was already prepared to leave a note. Which turned out to not be necessary, because as she reached the top of the driveway, there were both her mother and father's cars.

"You can do this, Mena," she said to herself as she turned off her engine and opened the car door. "You're only responsible for yourself. Your own actions. Not how you're received." She took a deep breath, let it out slowly and then stepped out of the car. She looked around being overtaken by all of the happy memories she had of playing in this yard, growing up in this house ... How many years had she wasted?

She began walking down the slate walkway toward the back door, but it opened before she got there.

"Wilhelmina?" her mother called out as she stepped onto the back porch. "Is that you?"

"It's me," Mena said, putting on a smile.

"Well ... this is certainly a surprise. Are you alright?"

Mena reached her mother and looked at her probably more closely than she had in a decade. Diana Weatherly was still beautiful. Age had not lessened that one bit. With only a slight hesitation, Mena put her arms around her mother and hugged her as tightly as her aching arm would allow.

"I love you, Mom. And I'm really sorry that I haven't shown it much in a long time," she whispered, surprised when she felt her mother return the hug.

"Wilhelmina, are you alright? Look at me," Diana said, stepping back just a little when the hug was over. "What's wrong? What happened to your arm?"

"Oh this ... I cut myself the other day. But it's okay." She gave her mother a smile that came a little more easily this time. "Can we talk? I only have a few minutes but ... there are some things I wanted you to know."

"Of course," her mother said, opening the back door and letting Mena go in first. She closed the door behind them and then hollered, "Pat? Wilhelmina's here!"

"Willie's here? I'm coming!" Patton Weatherly's voice emanated from some nearby room.

"Have a seat," Diana offered, motioning toward the kitchen table. "Is something wrong with Gemma?"

Mena shook her head. "No. As a matter of fact I was just with her. She's doing great in school."

Diana nodded her head, seemingly unsure of what to say next.

"Willie?" Pat said as he entered the kitchen. "Well ... this is a surprise."

Mena smiled. "That's what Mom said." She met her father halfway across the room and gave him a hug, like the one she had given to her mother. "I love you, Dad."

"I love you too. What are you doing down here?"

Mena went over to the kitchen table and sat down. "I just ... missed you. Both. I've been thinking a lot about how happy I was growing up and how hard you both worked. And Dad, I've been remembering all of our favorite songs. Mom ... I was thinking about that beautiful pink lipstick you used to wear. And how I hoped that someday I would marry a man that looked at me the way I'd always see Dad look at you when you didn't even know. How he'd glance over when he was driving and just... have this smile like he was the luckiest man in the world."

Diana and Pat stood together, watching their daughter. Not sure what to make of this unexpected and unusual visit.

"And ...?" her mother started, but didn't finish with anything else.

"And ... I didn't. Tyler was a good father and a good friend to me but ... we're getting divorced."

Her parents exchanged looks before they both walked over to the table and sat down.

"I'm really sorry to hear that, Willie," Pat said, sounding very sincere.

"Thank you, Dad. But I'm okay. In fact I was just talking to him about it and we're on the same page. Both of us just want to be good parents for Gemma and ... good people."

"And you can't do that together?" Diana asked.

"He's in love with someone else, Mom," Mena said, thinking somehow that explanation sounded more tasteful that he'd had sex with someone else.

There was silence for a moment before Pat asked, "Are you okay?"

Mena nodded. "I really am, Dad. I promise you."

"Is that why you came here today? Do you need somewhere to stay?" Diana asked.

"No, Mom," Mena answered. "Which brings me to the second thing I wanted to say. You asked me on the phone the other day what Jason Milstead wanted with me after the funeral."

Diana nodded.

"It was about the beach house."

"What beach house?" Pat asked.

"My grandfather's beach house. He never sold it. He's had it all of this time. And he left it to me. Well ... he asked me to go down and pack up his things ..."

"He asked ...?" Diana said, her voice a whisper.

"He'd given Jason a note to give to me after he passed."

"And you ...?"

"And that's where I've been for the last two weeks. Packing up his things and making repairs. Remember my interior design company that I sold?"

Diana nodded.

"Well I'm using that money to make the beach cottage into what he wanted. Apparently he talked about it all of the time with his neighbor ... his friend ... and the woman that runs the store ..."

"That store is still there?" Pat asked.

Mena nodded. "It is Dad. And it's just like I remembered."

"Are you ... going to sell it?" Diana asked softly.

Mena shook her head. "I've been wondering how I would feel ... if I'd be able to sell it when all of the work was done. But today ... today I finally know the answer. I can't. I can't sell it. And I want us to make new memories there. All of us. Our family. So I'm hoping that you two will come down next summer and … help us start over?" She reached her good hand across the table and covered her mother's. "What do you two say?"

"I'm game if your mother is," Pat said, rubbing his wife's back.

"Well you know what? You don't have to answer now. Just think about it. Because I've found out a lot of really wonderful things about your father, Mom. And I'd love to share it all with you. Whenever you're ready."

Mena stood up, leaning over to kiss her mother's cheek and then her father's. "I have to go, but I love you both. Very much. And thank you for … giving me this chance to be a better daughter to you."

"You've always been a great daughter," Pat said, with a nod. "Are you sure you have to go?"

She nodded. "I'm actually heading back down to Brandford now." She looked from one parent to the other. "I love you." And then she headed for the door.

"Wilhelmina?" her mother called after her.

Mena turned and looked at Diana.

"Will you send me a picture of the cottage?" she whispered.

"Of course I will. I have lots of pictures to send you."

Diana nodded. "Thank you."

"You be careful," Pat called after Mena as she walked out the back door.

When Mena returned to her car and pulled down the driveway, tears stung her eyes. But for once they were happy tears. Her relationship with her parents wasn't broken beyond repair. Maybe they had been cold. But maybe they could warm up again. And that was enough for her to know for now.

She looked down at her gas gauge and realized she should fill up before getting back onto 95. So she pulled into the next Wawa that she passed, taking her place at an open gas pump. She got out and paid, and then stood, holding the nozzle watching the numbers roll on the screen.

"Mena?"

She turned, not sure where the male voice calling her name was coming from. But then she saw Jason Milstead coming across the parking lot.

"I thought that was you," he said when he reached her car. "What are you doing in West Chester?"

Mena put the nozzle back on the pump and replaced her gas cap. "I was just visiting with my parents. How are you doing?"

"I'm good. Good. So … have you been to Brandford?" Jason asked.

"I have. In fact I'm heading back there now."

Jason smiled. "And … how has it been?"

Mena sighed. "It has been … everything that I needed. And so much more. I don't know how to explain it."

"You don't have to. Christopher would be so happy. This is what he wanted for you."

Mena's eyes widened. "Did he know?"

"Did he know what?"

"About me? About my husband? My marriage?"

Jason took a second but then he nodded. "He did. He had me … find you. He only had a few days left."

"But why me?" Mena whispered.

"I think he saw some of himself in you. He thought that out of everyone in his family, you needed Brandford the most. It made him sad that you lost your business. He said the cottage needed your … eye. Your touch. And with what your husband had done … he also secretly thought …"

"Chase," Mena said softly.

"Well … he knew he had no control over any of it. But … it was his last wish," Jason said. "Thank you for … honoring it."

Tears were in her eyes as she took out her phone. "Would you like to see it? The cottage?"

"I would," Jason answered, stepping closer so that he could see the many photos that Mena scrolled through for him. "So that's Brandford Beach," he said softly. "He must be so happy."

"I hope so," Mena answered, nodding. "I really do." Then she quickly gave the lawyer a hug. "Thank you. For … doing more for me than you could possibly imagine."

"It was all Chris. I was just the messenger," Jason said.

"Well … you're an amazing messenger. So thank you."

"You're very welcome, Mena. Call me? Let me know how you're doing?" he asked sincerely.

"I will. And when it's all finished, if you want to come down, you have a standing invitation."

"Thank you. I might just take you up on that."

"I hope that you do."

"Drive safe, Mena."

"I will. And thank you again, Jason."

"My pleasure."

Mena watched her grandfather's lawyer walk back across the parking lot and couldn't help but smile. "Well Christopher D'Angelo, you sly old dog, you." Her eyes turned upward toward the sky. "Thank you," she added in a whisper.

The closer Mena got to Brandford Beach, the more nervous she became. What if she couldn't fix what she'd done to her relationship with Chase? Or what if, like her own feelings for Tyler, he could forgive her but not resume their friendship. Just as she had thought he'd been dishonest with her, her reaction to Liz's bombshell could be something that maybe Chase could no longer deal with.

The air was crisp and the skies were the most brilliant shade of blue when she arrived. But her heart sank when she pulled onto Chase's street and it was empty. His truck was gone. Not feeling that she had the right to be a part of his house, she parked her car in front of the cottage as she had done that first day. But what a difference the weeks had made. The cottage was now raised, ready for the next steps to be taken in its renovation. Apparently work had continued, even though she'd been gone. She tried to picture what the cottage had looked like that first night. She took out her phone and scrolled again through her pictures until reaching that first one she sent to Gemma. What she wouldn't give to go back to that moment and be able to do it all over again. The right way.

She got out of her car and walked down to the beach, her eyes on her phone. She looked at the pictures she'd taken since she first arrived at Brandford Beach. Beautiful sunrises and sunsets. The smiles of her new friends. The handsome face of Chase Harper as he worked, cooked, and talked to her until all hours of the morning. Finally she had to face the possibility that just maybe the pain she'd inflicted on Chase might take more time to heal than only two days. Maybe, like Mena, he'd need to work through things at his own pace. In his own time.

Before putting her phone away she sent him a text: 'I came back in hopes of talking. I'm so sorry I missed you. Please call me.'

She tucked the phone into her pocket and started back toward her car. She froze when she saw his truck, and him standing next to it, his phone in his hand.

She didn't know what to do as she looked at him. Was he silently cursing himself for his own bad timing? Or just maybe could he be as glad to see her as she was to see him? She only felt like her strength to move her feet had returned when he took a few steps away from his truck, toward her.

She took the first few steps slowly, but picked up the pace. Suddenly unable to reach him fast enough. When she was finally in front of him she couldn't keep herself from throwing her arms around his neck, leaning against him.

"I'm so sorry," she said. "I can't apologize enough, Chase. I don't know what was wrong with me. You deserved so much better!"

Chase stood quietly, but she felt him move one arm around her back. Holding her gently.

She pulled back enough to look at his face, seeing the effect her betrayal had on him. His eyes were red and slightly swollen. "Can you forgive me?"

Chase looked surprised by her question. "Forgive you?"

She nodded. "You have been nothing but kind and generous to me and I acted like a spoiled child because you didn't tell me something so personal. In the time I wanted you to tell me."

"I should have told y—"

Mena put a finger against Chase's lips.

"No," she said. "We were friends, Chase. For only a few weeks. And while I felt so close to you so quickly, that doesn't mean it was enough time for you to maybe feel comfortable enough sharing absolutely everything with me. Just because I ran at the mouth about every little thing in my life, does not give me the right to expect the same from you. It wasn't like you'd asked me to marry you while keeping secrets. And I wasn't a good friend. A good friend wouldn't have reacted that way. A good friend would have gone to you to ask if you wanted to talk about it." Mena smiled. "Or maybe a good friend would have stopped Liz from telling me something you obviously didn't want me to know yet."

"She was just trying to help," Chase said quietly, his lips moving against Mena's finger.

She laughed, pulling her hand away. "She was." She took Chase's hand and sat down in one of his lawn chairs, urging him to sit beside her. When he did she looked at his profile. "You haven't answered me yet? Do you think you'll be able to forgive me?" she asked softly.

"There's nothing to forgive, Mena," Chase answered. "You asked for honesty and I didn't give it to you."

She shook her head. "But that's not true. If I'd asked you straight up if you'd been responsible for what happened to your grandfather and you said 'no', that would be a slight deviation from the truth," she said with a smile. "You didn't rewrite history. You didn't replace any facts. You just chose to leave the more painful details out. Which was absolutely your right to do at the time."

He was quiet for a moment before looking over at her. "But when you left, I just assumed ..."

"I was always going to make the trip home. Tyler and I started our divorce moving forward. The paperwork is being drawn up and we talked to Gem. I'd finally got my courage up to just ... get it done. I was afraid to not go. Afraid my head might turn against me again."

"So you really made your decision?"

She smiled. "I'd made it a long time ago, I just ... was too scared to end what was familiar and ... safe."

"But now?"

"Now ... I'm excited about closing my eyes and taking the leap into whatever the future holds. The only thing that kept me from being completely happy about what I'd done was ... worrying about us. If I'd ruined the best relationship I'd ever had with someone."

Chase shook his head. "You didn't ruin anything. And I'm glad you're happy. You deserve to be."

"And so do you. But ... I don't think I've ever seen you look more unhappy. Tell me what I can do to fix this," she said, sounding like Tyler had the day before.

He shook his head. "You didn't do anything wrong so there's nothing to fix. Honestly."

They sat side by side, now looking straight ahead toward Christopher's house. Without looking over at him, Mena reached her good hand over, her palm up. Chase glanced down and then at her face. She slowly turned to look at him.

"Do you still think you could love me?" she whispered.

"I do," he answered with a smile, wrapping his hand around hers.

EPILOGUE

"Chase! Gem's here. Come on!" Mena hollered, drying her hands on the towel that was laying on the corner of the island. She hurried to the door, waiting for Chase to come in from the deck. She held her hand out, smiling when he took it in his own, closing his fingers around it. It was a feeling that she couldn't imagine would ever get old.

"I love you," he said softly.

She smiled, moving closer, leaning up so that she could place a soft kiss against his lips. "I love you too," she said, her eyes sparkling.

He lifted her hand, admiring the ring that she now wore. The ring that showed the world she'd agreed to be his wife. He kissed her hand softly.

"Okay. I'm ready," he said with a smile of his own.

The two opened the door and walked down the stairs, Mena running ahead to pull Gemma into a tight hug that was returned instantly.

"Oh I missed you so much!" Mena said against her daughter's hair.

"I missed you too, Mom," Gemma said before untangling herself from her mother's embrace. "Mom, I want you to meet Wesley. Wesley, this is my Mom. Mena."

Mena couldn't smile any bigger when she let go of her daughter and focused instead on the young man that was still standing by his car.

"Wesley," she said. "It's so nice to finally meet you. I feel like I know you already from all that Gemma's told me … I'm so happy that you were able to come with her." She met the man halfway and gave him a hug as well. Then she turned to the incredible man that was still standing nervously at the bottom of the staircase. "And I want to introduce you both to Chase Harper," she said with a proud smile. "My fiance and newly published author."

"Wait! Are you serious? Fiance?" Gemma squealed. "Congratulations! How could you keep this a secret?" She first hugged her mother tight, admiring the engagement ring. Then she walked over to Chase and put her arms around him. "Thank you for making my mom so happy," she said.

"It's been my pleasure," Chase answered emotionally, looking over Gemma's head to Mena who had tears in her eyes. "And it's nice to finally see you face to face."

Gemma stood back, Mena and Wesley walking over to her and Chase.

"So this is Chase's house," Mena said, "And that … that is Christopher's cottage," she said, pointing across the street to the beautiful home that Chase had finished for her.

"It really is perfect," Gemma said. "It looks even prettier than in the pictures. Have you decided what you're going to do with it? Are you going to sell it?"

Mena shook her head, taking Chase's hand again. "Never. In fact, your grandparents are actually going to come down and stay there for a few days in July."

"Well I can't wait for the tour," Gemma said.

"We can walk over after dinner," Mena promised. "And I'll catch you up on everything."

"Oh man! I have to get back up to the grill before everything burns!" Chase said, turning quickly for the stairs.

"Come on everybody, let's get you settled and then give you the treat of one of Chase's delicious meals," Mena said with a little laugh. "After you."

"I can see why you fell in love with this place," Gemma said as she walked past her mother. "I'd want to stay too." She took Wesley's hand and the two walked up the stairs side by side. Mena heard Gemma ask, "So you wrote a book? ..." before they reached the deck.

Mena turned to follow but saw a movement out of the corner of her eye. She turned and saw her neighbor, walking down from the beach. She reached up her arm to wave. "Hi Ron! Happy Memorial Day!"

"Happy Memorial Day, Mena. I think it's going to be a great summer!"

Mena felt like her smile might just split her face in two. "Oh so do I!"

She turned and hurried up the stairs, following the sounds of the happy voices of the people she loved. "Here I come!" she called out.

ABOUT THE AUTHOR

Lyn Corvet has been writing for her own enjoyment, and that of friends and family, for most of her life. It wasn't until the Covid shutdown that she entertained the thought of actually self publishing one of her many stories. Her approach to writing is simply to provide a literary escape for readers. Something that writing has always been for her. She is a fan of the happy ending, but takes time to explore the emotional journeys that lead from pain to joy, and the relationships that help support the characters throughout that journey. Lyn cites her own most important relationships as the ones she has with her two amazing daughters, and her sister/best friend that instilled in her a love of music and books at an early age. That love has only grown with time and is probably why you'll always find music to be a main character in any of Lyn's novels.

ALSO AVAILABLE